The sound of his voice vibrated huskily in her ears, and she took a deep, quivering breath. Her flesh tingled where her hands rested in his, and she could smell the clean male scent of him, both sensations combining to make her mind spin crazily. She said the first thing that popped into her head.

"You didn't ask my permission this morning."

Lance laughed softly. "I wasn't on my best behavior this morning."

"Are you now?" The tip of her pink tongue darted out nervously to moisten dry lips, inadvertantly drawing his gaze.

"That depends on you," he murmured warmly, eyes lingering on her mouth.

Her lips were parted in silent provocation, tawny eyes wide and uncertain as they were drawn helplessly upward to his. Jami was never able to remember exactly when the touch of his lips was no longer a memory but a reality, a reality she wished would go on forever . . .

WHAT ARE *LOVESWEPT* ROMANCES?

They are stories of true romance and touching emotion. We believe those two very important ingredients are constants in our highly sensual and very believable stories in the *LOVESWEPT* line. Our goal is to give you, the reader, stories of consistently high quality that may sometimes make you laugh, sometimes make you cry, but are always fresh and creative and contain many delightful surprises within their pages.

Most romance fans read an enormous number of books. Those they truly love, they keep. Others may be traded with friends and soon forgotten. We hope that each *LOVESWEPT* romance will be a treasure—a "keeper." We will always try to publish

LOVE STORIES YOU'LL NEVER FORGET
BY AUTHORS YOU'LL ALWAYS REMEMBER

The Editors

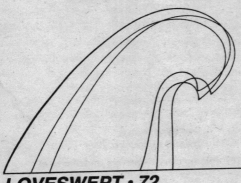

LOVESWEPT · 72

Sandra Kleinschmit
Probable Cause

 BANTAM BOOKS
TORONTO · NEW YORK · LONDON · SYDNEY · AUCKLAND

PROBABLE CAUSE

A Bantam Book / December 1984

LOVESWEPT and the wave device are trademarks of
Bantam Books, Inc.

ISBN 0-553-21687-2

Published simultaneously in the United States and Canada

Bantam Books are published by Bantam Books, Inc. Its
trademark, consisting of the words "Bantam Books" and
the portrayal of a rooster, is Registered in U.S. Patent and
Trademark Office and in other countries. Marca Registrada.
Bantam Books, Inc., 666 Fifth Avenue, New York, New
York 10103.

PRINTED IN THE UNITED STATES OF AMERICA

O   0 9 8 7 6 5 4 3 2 1

Chapter One

"Is your life insurance paid up, mister? If not, I wouldn't bat so much as an eyelash if I were you!"

The first misty gray fingers of dawn were stealing upward to pearl the morning sky as the voice flitted out of the darkness, cool and steady and betraying not the slightest quiver of fear. Officer Jami Simpson stood poised and ready to shoot as her prisoner made a jerky, evasive movement, but he froze into immobility as another, more deadly sound penetrated the early morning air—the sound of a trigger being cocked.

"Don't even *think* of trying to get away," she informed the man in a voice no less lethal because of its soft, silky quality. A sudden vision of Clint Eastwood in his *Dirty Harry* role came to mind, and

1

she couldn't resist an added threat. "Maybe you feel lucky and think you can outrun a bullet from a .357 Magnum. Believe me, it can't be done."

"Don't get trigger-happy, lady, I'm not about to try." The broad-shouldered figure looming in front of her suddenly seemed to have found his voice. "Why don't you put that gun away?"

"Not quite yet. I need to find out what's going on here."

A taut silence reigned for a tension-filled moment. "I suppose you think I'm trying to break into this building," the man finally said.

"It looks that way, doesn't it," Jami stated coolly, a sarcastic edge to her voice.

"You're making a big mistake here, lady." The man glanced over his shoulder, eyes widening slightly as he saw the small, uniformed figure behind him. He began turning toward her, but Jami raised the barrel of her gun and ordered, "Hands up!"

"All right, all right!" He immediately complied, but from the sudden darkening of his expression she could see he clearly didn't want to. In fact, he looked to Jami as though he believed that if he could get away with it, he'd waste no time disarming her.

But Jami was too much of a professional to let that happen. "Suppose you tell me exactly what you're doing here," she said.

"I was trying to get inside this building—"

"That much is obvious! I watched you for several minutes fiddling with the doorknob. What I want to know is what's inside that you're so anxious to get to."

The man made absolutely no effort to answer, choosing instead to glare at her. Jami was used to such reactions from felons and petty thieves, however. They seldom readily admitted their guilt. She glanced at the low brick building and back to the man.

"This is a doctor's office, you know."

"I'm very well aware of that," he bit out through clenched teeth.

Jami merely smiled at his hostile attitude. The man was clearly put out because he'd been caught in the act of breaking and entering, by none other than a police officer, and a female one at that! She could just imagine the insults that were running through his mind.

"Don't be shy now," she said cajolingly. "Tell me what you were after." When he remained silent, she speculated aloud. "Office equipment?" No, a quick glance around the parking area revealed no vehicle to stow it in. She decided on the most logical motive. "Were you planning to steal some drugs?"

At the grim tightening of his mouth and the flicker of thick dark lashes, she smiled to herself in satisfaction. She had her answer.

Her gaze took in the man's blond hair, straight aquiline nose, and firm mouth, then swept over his tall, well-built body and returned to his face. Damn, but the man was attractive! He had to be one of the best-looking men she'd ever seen in her life, and this from a woman who rarely gave a man a second glance!

All beside the point, however. Jami brought herself back to the subject at hand almost reluctantly. "Are you a user?"

"A what?" He sounded absolutely incredulous.

"You know," she said irritably. "A drug user—a junkie."

"Hell, no!" he shouted.

Jami nodded to herself. Somehow she'd suspected he wasn't a user. The only other reason he'd be intent upon stealing drugs from a doctor's office was patently obvious—he intended to sell them. Her lips tightened angrily as she realized that this man very possibly depended on school-age youngsters for a ready supply of cash. He preyed on the weaknesses of children who were little more than babies—and she had no use for him.

The light of condemnation flared in the tawny-gold depths of her eyes as she commanded, "Hands up against the wall, feet spread apart."

Again he glowered at her and shook his blond head, making no move to do as she requested. "I'm telling you I wasn't trying to break into this building. This isn't—"

"Just do it, mister! *Now!*" Who the hell did he think he was? Jami widened her own stance threateningly, tightening both slim hands around the handle of her revolver. Small and delicate she might be, but she was a crack shot.

This time he obeyed, placing his long tapered hands against the smooth brick wall and backing away slightly, but not before an even more frigid mask descended over his handsome features. He was cool as a cucumber, Jami thought disgustedly. Clearly this was hardly a new experience for him.

She replaced her weapon in the holster and stepped up to him. "Okay, let's see if you're hiding anything."

"You're going to *search* me?" The deep male voice was heavily shaded with disbelief, along with some other emotion. Anger? Probably, she decided, not in the least perturbed. She supposed it was only natural, considering she was in the process of depriving him of his day's cash flow.

"Of course I'm going to search you," she answered calmly. What did he expect, for heaven's sake? That she would let him go with a mere slap on the hands, just *hoping* he didn't spring a gun on her the minute her back was turned? She was becoming a little annoyed with his game-playing. He was carrying the innocent act a little too far.

She glared at the back of his well-shaped head as a thought flitted through her mind. What was such a good-looking man doing earning a living as a small-time drug pusher? If he was of a mind to do something sordid, he could probably earn a very tidy sum as the so-called "companion" of some wealthy woman in need of stud services. Not that Oregon's capital city boasted an overabundance of such poor creatures, but surely there were greener pastures to the south. Los Angeles, San Francisco . . .

Her small hand wasn't particularly gentle as she reached up and grabbed his left shoulder, but she knew she couldn't inflict much damage through the thick sheepskin of his coat. One booted foot stretched out to further widen his stance as she nudged his feet into the position she favored for frisking suspects, his body bent forward at nearly a forty-five degree angle.

"Whoever said a woman's touch was soft and gentle sure as hell never met you," the man muttered, just loud enough for Jami to hear.

"And if you were any kind of a *man*, you wouldn't

be in the business you're in!" The retort sprang from her lips before she could prevent it.

"Is that so?"

"Yes, that's so! And please stop swearing, you might burn my tender ears!"

There was a definite smirk in his voice as he said, "I don't think there's anything I could say that you haven't heard before."

Now *there* was something she couldn't take exception to. The people with whom she was forced to keep company while on duty weren't particularly disposed to subtlety, especially when it came to praising her womanly attributes. Not that she expected any such praise from *this* man. For some reason, they seemed to grate against each other like a fingernail scraping a chalkboard.

"You're really going to go through with this, aren't you?" He threw her an accusing gaze over one broad shoulder.

"I told you I would, didn't I?"

"Yes, but I didn't think you'd actually *do* it."

"Mister, unlike you, I don't say things I don't mean," she informed him calmly.

"So now you're calling me a liar on top of treating me like a criminal of the worst kind!" The man's voice had deepened dangerously, and Jami was well aware that the low tone signaled an emotion that went far deeper than frustration at being foiled.

It was, perhaps, again time to put him in his place. "As far as I'm concerned, a criminal is what you are. Attempted burglary happens to be a felony in this state, in case you didn't know," she emphasized. "And in case you've forgotten, I happen to be in charge here, whether you like it or not!"

"I don't like it, lady," the man growled, "but since you've got a gun, there isn't much I can do about it."

"I'm glad you're finally beginning to see the light." It suddenly struck her that she was baiting him, and enjoying it too. She really wasn't quite sure why—normally she was the soul of integrity while on duty.

"You won't find anything on me," he informed her stonily, as if by this simple proclamation he could persuade her to abandon her resolve.

"We'll see about that," she said smugly. "Besides, mister, in my line of work—"

"The name is Morgan. Lance Morgan."

There was a cryptically expectant look in his eye that made her wonder if she was supposed to know him. Was he wanted by the FBI or something? She continued as if he hadn't spoken. "—in my line of work I can't afford to give anyone the benefit of the doubt."

"Not even a law-abiding citizen like me?" he asked mockingly.

"Especially a *so-called* law-abiding citizen like you. Now if you don't mind, *Mister* Morgan," she said with a downward curl of her lips, "I'm going to—"

"It's not *Mister*, it's—"

"Look, I don't care if it's *Ms.*, *Mrs.*, or *Miss*, I don't have time to argue with you about what you want me to call you," she cut in sharply. "The sooner I search you, the sooner I can arrest you and take you to the station, and the sooner you can post your bail and be on your way. Only the next time you make up your mind to ply your trade, you'd better look over your shoulder first because I'm liable to be right behind you!" It was a hollow threat, but she couldn't resist the jab.

"I'd like to ply my trade with you, all right," he muttered viciously under his breath.

Jami caught the words and finally let loose her temper. "This is the last time I'm going to tell you! Cut the gab or you'll be looking at a disorderly conduct charge in addition to attempted burglary!"

The man opened his mouth, then clamped his jaw shut with a snap. If looks could burn, Jami suspected there would be a gaping hole the size of a basketball in the brick wall that was bearing the brunt of his gaze.

Several things hovered in the back of her mind, however, as she prepared to search him. He hardly fit the stereotype of a typical burglar. For one thing, he was too old—mid-thirties, she guessed—and there was a keenly intelligent edge to what she suspected was normally a smooth, well-modulated voice. He was clearly no pro, but even the rankest amateur would have more sense than to attempt a break-in at dawn's first light. The risk of being seen was far greater than in the dead of night.

Jami's slim hands slid over his arms, then reached around to the front of his body to search for concealed weapons. His jacket was open and she patted down his torso. Though she tried to remain impassive, she was suddenly conscious of the lean and contoured flesh under the thin material of his shirt. Damn, but the man was in the wrong business! The long, lean body and strong chiseled features were even getting to *her*, quite a feat in light of the fact that men barely existed for her.

They were fine as coworkers—they had to be since there were only four women among Salem's one-hundred-thirty or so sworn officers—but thus far in her twenty-six years, no man had managed to pique more than a mild interest. And the few men she'd met on her off-duty hours seemed to have a very hard time dealing with her occupation. Once they found out she was a police officer . . . Well, that seemed to send them scurrying for cover in a hurry . . . a *big* hurry!

Nor was her opinion of the male of the species bolstered by the troublesome fact that they seemed to have an amazingly narrow set of interests. Sex and sports—sports and sex! That was all her fellow partners against crime ever talked about—or bragged about—while gathering for briefings.

With a sense of irritation Jami resumed her task. The general policy was for male officers to search men and for female officers to search women, but the shift was short of personnel today. One officer was on vacation and two others were out with the flu.

Jami was confident of her ability to handle both the man and the situation. She was shocked to realize, though, that she was only too aware of this stranger as a man, a very attractive man, and she had to remind herself forcibly that he was a criminal. She'd never had this particular reaction before and she decided that after three years on the force, she must be getting soft.

Bending slightly at the waist, she ran both hands up and down the length of one sinewy leg and then the other. Her fingers hovered for just an instant around his knee and she glanced up, unable to suppress a grin.

Better brace yourself, Lance Morgan, she warned him silently. *If you're as innocent as you say you are, this might come as quite a shock!*

Straightening, she encircled his waist once again

and slid her fingers along the inside of his belt. Then, taking a deep breath, she reached around to the front of his body and patted down the area directly below his belt buckle, her touch firm and sure.

Jami almost laughed aloud at his quick intake of breath, but her smile rapidly faded. She could feel something! Yes, he was definitely hiding some object down the front of his slacks!

"Are you sure you know what you're doing?" the man complained in a voice that sounded odd, rather strangled.

"Of course I do," she muttered, intent upon her task.

"Then will you *please* get it over with!" He clearly had no more liking for this part of the search than she did, his voice growing louder and more impatient with each word.

"Take it easy. I'm almost through." Jami shot a quelling look at the back of his head and again probed the area. Suddenly she jerked her hand back as if she'd been seared by a blow torch, eyes widening in horror and embarrassment as she took a giant step backward. Lord, she'd never had *this* happen!

"All right," she mumbled, hardly daring to look at him as she felt her cheeks grow hot. "You can relax now, you're clean."

"Now do you see, why I wanted you to hurry?" He glanced over at her, then down at the front of his slacks, disgust clearly stamped on his handsome features. But whether it was aimed at himself or at her, Jami couldn't be sure.

Nor did she care. It was disconcerting enough to have discovered that he was unequivocally and undeniably a man, in the fullest sense of the word, and in perfect working order. What she'd thought might well be the handle or barrel of a weapon had been . . . well, hardly that.

"If you search men like that very often, you're lucky you haven't been raped by now!" He sent a withering glance in her direction. "I've heard of men trying to cop a feel from a woman, but the other way around?" Again he shook his head, then suddenly chuckled as he realized his pun. When he finally stopped laughing, he looked at her, his deep blue eyes glinting with humor for the first time. "Don't you have a partner around to do the dirty work?"

Jami's eyes narrowed. She disliked being the object of this man's ridicule, and she certainly didn't need him telling her how to do her job. The man might be a thief, but somehow she knew he didn't pose any real threat to her safety—now that she'd discovered he wasn't carrying any weapons.

"I don't need any help with scum like you," she said stiffly, lifting her delicate chin as she reached for the snap on her handcuff case. She pulled out the cuffs and dangled them in front of him. His blue eyes hardened to two brittle chips of ice, but she met the chilly look with one of her own. "Now be a good boy and turn around so I can put these pretty bracelets on you," she said sweetly.

"Oh, no, you don't!" Before she had any inkling of what he was up to, the man had fastened steely fingers around her slender wrist and was hauling her around the side of the small building. There was no time to panic or to reach for either her gun or her radio before he came to a halt near the front corner of the building.

"See that?" He dropped her wrist as if touching her

was suddenly distasteful to him and stabbed a finger toward a large wooden sign standing upright in a narrow patch of grass and shrubbery. "Maybe you'd like to prove to me that you can read as well as shoot your mouth off!"

Jami was too flabbergasted by his unexpected actions to pay attention to his cutting words. Following the direction of his finger, her large amber eyes flitted to the ornate lettering carved into the dark wood, and what she saw there made her gasp. The sign said Lance Morgan, M.D., Internal Medicine.

She could only stare in confused shock for a moment. Then her eyes darted to his face and she suddenly recalled his expectant look when he'd told her his name. Oh, no, what had she done . . . But no, she couldn't take any chances. He *could* be lying.

"This doesn't prove anything, you know," she said quickly. "You could have seen this sign before you went around to the back to break in. Claiming to be this doctor doesn't prove you *are.*" She held out her hand and said crisply, "I'll need to see some identification."

"You are the most suspicious person I have ever encountered in my entire life," he muttered savagely, glaring at her as he reached into his back pocket and extracted a brown leather wallet. "Here." He thrust a small rectangular card into her upturned palm.

It was a driver's license. The morning sun peeked out from behind a dismal gray cloud, highlighting the strands of gold in his hair. Jami looked up from the picture on the license to the man standing so rigidly in front of her. Yes, it was the same person, the same name. There was no mistaking the thick dark brows that slashed above those crystal blue eyes and contrasted so sharply with the sunstreaked hair falling onto his tanned forehead, no mistaking the bold nose and the firm mouth.

She, Jami Simpson, with an absolutely perfect record as a police officer, had very nearly arrested a doctor who was merely trying to get into his own office! A horrible sinking sensation formed in the pit of her stomach, but it was tempered by the knowledge that it wasn't entirely her fault.

"You could have told me, you know," she said through stiff lips, a blaze of defiance lighting her eyes to a golden brown.

"I tried, remember?" His gaze was stony as it clashed with hers.

"Not very hard, you didn't."

"Lady," he said, forming the word with a precision that was far from flattering, "you had a gun pointed at my back and it seemed to me you were pretty damn anxious to use it. What did you want me to do?"

"I was not anxious to use it!" Jami protested. "You can hardly expect me to saunter up behind you and say 'Hey, there' "—her voice turned brittle as she crossed her arms over her dark blue jacket and looked up at him—" 'you're under arrest for attempted burglary,' with no thought for my own protection! For all I knew, you could have pulled a gun on *me* when you turned around!"

"You had me up against the wall frisking me before I ever got the chance to turn around. What were you looking for anyway?"

Not liking his attitude at all, Jami said coolly, "I just told you, Dr. Morgan. A gun, razor blades . . ."

Lance Morgan's brows shot upward in sheer disbelief. "Razor blades!" he exclaimed. "Do you honestly think I'd be carrying razor blades in my—" He stopped short, and Jami was profoundly grateful he didn't continue. The whole case of mistaken identity was embarrassing enough without adding to it his body's response to her touch. He sent her a scathing look. "Lord, woman, I'm not crazy! I have absolutely no desire to find myself a eunuch!"

Color flooded Jami's cheeks, but she forced herself to meet his accusing glare. "I thought I felt something that might have been a weapon," she defended herself. "I had to make sure."

"A weapon?" He sounded utterly disgusted. "Exactly what kind of weapon?"

"The—the barrel of a revolver or the handle of a knife," she said, distinctly uncomfortable with the subject.

"The barrel of a revolver? The handle of a knife?" He threw back his head and laughed, the hearty sound startling Jami. "I don't know whether to be insulted or flattered."

"You aren't supposed to be either," she muttered, gritting her teeth. Though the sound of his laughter was like his voice, low and pleasing to the ear—when he wasn't shouting—it grated on her nerves. She stood with her head angled defiantly as she waited for a snappy comeback, but there was none.

Lance let his gaze sweep slowly over the small figure before him, watching as she replaced the handcuffs in the case with a snap, noting that even with her ebony hair piled into a loose knot on the crown of her head, she barely reached his chin.

Jami was very much aware of the bold gaze raking her slim form. It mattered little to her that her uniform completely hid her feminine curves, that the bulletproof vest she wore under the dark blue shirt nearly flattened her small breasts, or that the wide gunbelt circling her hips effectively concealed a very trim waistline.

But when his eyes lifted to her delicate features, his earlier amusement was gone, as was the taut set of the clean-shaven jaw and the derisive twist of his lips. Yet the deep blue eyes betrayed no clue as to what he was thinking, and Jami breathlessly found herself wishing she could see into his mind.

"I could report you for this, you know," he said slowly, his gaze again wandering over her body.

She drew a deep breath. So that explained the expression on his face. At least now she knew what he'd been contemplating while giving her the once-over—revenge and retaliation. Somehow the knowledge that he hadn't seen beyond the uniform and badge to the woman within was—disappointing.

Suppressing these thoughts, she shrugged in what she hoped was a nonchalant way. "Go ahead," she said.

Lance Morgan raised an eyebrow. "You don't care if I file a complaint about your near-arrest of an innocent man?"

"I can't say I relish the idea." Actually, she hated it! Being called in for a nice little chat with Sergeant Nelson in Internal Affairs was hardly the highlight of an officer's day. "But," she added in all honesty, "I really don't think your complaint will get you anything but the momentary satisfaction of letting off some steam. The charge will be investigated. But sustained? I'm afraid I don't think so."

"And why is that?" The soft voice was almost a threat.

Jami rocked back on her heels, again preparing to do battle. She wasn't about to allow him to intimidate her. "Because," she said with a smug smile, "I saw you fiddling with that doorknob for almost five minutes before I came up behind you. You kept looking around and pushing against the door with your shoulder. Rather suspicious actions for a man who supposedly has a legitimate reason for entering a building, wouldn't you say?"

"No." Again he fixed her with a cool look. "Not when I couldn't get my key in the lock."

"Oh, come on." She couldn't hold back a laugh. "Can't you come up with anything better than that?"

"It happens to be the truth," he said coldly. "At six-fifteen in the morning it's still dark outside, or hadn't you noticed, Officer?" The last words dripped sarcasm.

At least he'd refrained from calling her "lady" in that irritating manner. She was just about to let loose a very *un*ladylike term for this infuriating man when he stepped up to her and tapped the end of her nose with a lean finger.

"Try to use a little more finesse the next time you search an unsuspecting male," he said in a softly mocking voice. "Your next victim may not have the superb control that I had."

Speechless, Jami watched with a suppressed fury as he strode away from her and rounded the corner. Lance Morgan was, without a doubt, the most irritating, exasperating, annoying man she had ever had the misfortune to come up against—*and* the most gorgeous!

Chapter Two

Jami's thoughts were once again on her work as she walked briskly toward the alley where her squad car was parked. But as she reached for the car keys she'd hooked onto her Sam Browne belt, she discovered they weren't there.

"Oh, no!" She groaned. "Don't tell me I've done it again!"

She quickened her pace to a dead run, halting beside the light blue squad car and trying vainly to open the door. It was locked, as she had known it would be. She *always* locked it when she had to leave the vehicle. Peering inside, she discovered that her initial suspicion had been correct. The keys were lying on the seat, hopelessly unattainable.

Groaning again, she turned and sagged against the

hood, trying to decide between two disagreeable choices. It was either radio her plight to headquarters, inviting the laughter of her coworkers since it was the second time in the past two weeks she'd locked herself out of her car—or ask Lance Morgan for help. She wasn't the first officer to have made such a stupid mistake and she knew she wouldn't be the last, but the thought was little comfort.

Scowling, she made a quick decision and retraced her steps. The door of the office building was unlocked so Jami stepped inside, glancing down the narrow hallway. Spotting a light in one of the rooms, she quickly walked to it and knocked softly on the half-open door, poised on the threshold of what was obviously Lance Morgan's office.

He was seated behind an oaken rolltop desk reading a medical record, but he looked up at her knock.

"Now what? Don't tell me you're here to try to arrest me again."

Jami stiffened at his tone. "Hardly," she retorted coolly. "I was wondering if there might be a wire coat hanger I could borrow."

"A what?"

"A wire coat hanger," she repeated, dropping her gaze and feeling very foolish indeed. First she had nearly arrested an innocent man, and now she was asking that same man to help her break into her squad car. She was only too aware she was hardly giving a good impression of Salem's finest.

Pride stiffened her upper lip, though, as Lance Morgan gave a low chuckle. "You locked yourself out of your car," he said with amusement. "And you don't have a spare set of keys."

"The station does. *I* don't."

"But you'd rather not have to contact the station." He got up and stood in front of her. Crossing his arms over his chest, he looked down at her, making Jami feel for all the world like a child who'd just been caught with her hand in the cookie jar.

But the feeling subsided as another took its place. She noticed he had removed his coat and her eyes were confirming what her hands had already discovered—his shoulders were wide, his hips lean and narrow, his entire body taut and muscular, without an inch of spare flesh to mar the splendid physique.

Her gaze flickered away from the disturbing sight of his body, then returned to his face as he spoke.

"I really ought to let you take the other way out of this."

"Fine, I'll do that," Jami muttered, whirling away from the mocking voice and eyes. She was beginning to discover that a little of Lance Morgan went a long, long way! She turned on her heel and was about to march into the hallway when a hand on her arm stopped her.

Jami looked up into Lance's face, furious, but he only laughed and reached for his coat before releasing her hand. Then he extracted a coat hanger from a closet behind him and handed it to her.

Jami's voice bore no trace of graciousness as she muttered "thank you" and continued on her way out.

She halted at the building's entrance, however, as she realized Lance Morgan apparently had every intention of coming with her.

Lips puckered with annoyance, she stared up at him. "I don't need a watchdog, you know. I can manage very well by myself."

"I think I'd better see for myself," he said, arching a dark eyebrow and putting his coat on. "You don't seem to be managing very well this morning."

"So tell me something I don't already know," Jami muttered. It was hard to believe that only an hour ago she'd thought the day was going to go so well. She'd only been out of the station fifteen minutes when she'd spied Lance Morgan and had started looking forward to chalking up her first arrest of the day. Well, she'd learned her lesson—she wouldn't be so optimistic from now on.

She was conscious of his presence behind her as she strode toward the car, straightening the coat hanger as she walked. But try as she would, she had no success in maneuvering the end of the coat hanger inside the door frame to unhook the lock. She became so absorbed in the task that she completely forgot Lance was behind her. When she finally turned in dismay, she very nearly poked him in the stomach with the pointed end of the coat hanger.

With a muttered oath, he stepped clear. "Lord, woman, you don't need to carry a gun. Just give you a coat hanger and you'll be armed to the hilt!"

"I'm sorry, really." Somehow she didn't sound very apologetic as she tried unsuccessfully to hold back a smile.

He gave her a withering look and took the coat hanger from her hand. "Here, I'll do it. We're both liable to be here all day if I leave it to you."

Jami stepped back willingly. She couldn't decide which was worse—an angry Lance Morgan or a mocking Lance Morgan, and she couldn't help wondering what he was like when he was neither. As the thought flashed through her mind, she felt her own defenses against him slipping.

He unlocked the door with no trouble at all and opened it with a flourish, a smile of self-satisfaction tipping the corners of his mouth. His blond hair whipping in the chill January breeze gave him a boyish look and he suddenly seemed . . . more approachable.

"Thanks a lot," Jami said, her soft mouth unconsciously curving into a dazzling smile. She was totally unaware of Lance's quick intake of breath as his gaze took in the peach-tinted flush staining her high cheekbones and the small white teeth revealed by her parted lips.

"If I didn't know better," she added, "I'd think you earned your way through medical school this way."

"How?" A puzzled frown etched its way between his brows.

"By breaking into cars, stealing the contents, and then selling them," she responded teasingly.

"Thanks for the vote of confidence," he said, "but I guess it's better late than never." He caught her arm as she made a move to enter the car. "What's your name?"

"Simpson." She pointed to the name tag on her dark blue jacket.

"No, your first name," he said, his voice unexpectedly soft.

Her gaze was drawn upward to his in surprise and, strangely enough, pleasure. But the blue eyes were subjecting her to a scrutiny that suddenly made her feel like an insect under a microscopic examination. She hesitated a moment before she finally said, "Jami."

"Jami Simpson," he repeated, and her stomach fluttered faintly. The way he'd said her name—so softly, almost caressingly—made her body feel all shivery inside. Nor did it help matters when his gaze skimmed over her slim form from head to toe, lingering on the swell of her breasts, or rather where the swell *should* have been. She had the fleeting feeling that he was mentally stripping away the layers of her bulky clothing.

"What would you say if I asked you out?" he asked suddenly.

"Asked me out!" Jami's heart felt as if it were temporarily lodged in her throat. "*Are* you asking?"

"Maybe." He smiled a rather secretive and lazy smile, pushing his hands into the pockets of his dark brown slacks and surveying her through lashes that were incredibly long and thick for a man.

Jami's heart suddenly dropped to her stomach. He was up to something, she knew it, she just knew it! First he'd been angry and upset with her for trying to arrest him, then he'd mocked her and laughed at her, and now—

"Are you making a pass?" she demanded.

"You don't believe in beating around the bush, do you?" He gave her another cryptic smile. "What if I were?"

"I'd say it was only to get back at me somehow." Her quick mind was off and running in a flash. "To—exact retribution. Or maybe you think I owe you something for mistaking you for a burglar."

"You're not about to boost anyone's ego, not even your own," he observed, still smiling. Jami began to wonder why they were even having this totally ridiculous conversation. "You really are a suspicious woman," he added softly. "But back to the point in question—what would you do if I *were* making a pass?"

What kind of game was he playing? Jami had no idea, but she did know it was time it came to a screeching halt. "My reaction," she said, bristling, "would be the same as it always is when someone makes a pass while I'm on duty." And there had been a number of them, at least three or four a week. "I'd ignore it, or tell you where to get off."

But would she? *Of course*, said a small voice, only to be negated by another, more insistent one which told her she'd have welcomed his attention. Either way, she told herself firmly, it didn't matter, because he was posing a purely hypothetical question. "Anyway," she added aloud without really knowing quite why, "even if you did ask me out and I wanted to accept, I couldn't."

"Why not?"

"When we're on duty, we're not—"

"Allowed to fraternize with the enemy?" he finished knowingly.

"Well, yes." She squinted up at him through the hazy sunlight. "Although I suppose you're not exactly the enemy."

Lance was quiet for a moment, and Jami looked up to find the smile gone from his face. A strange light was flickering in the back of his eyes, and somehow she knew that whatever his game was, it was at an end.

"I won't say it's been a pleasure," he said, moving closer and blocking out the sun's shimmery light, "at least not the *entire* time we've spent in each other's company, but I will say it's been—memorable."

There was little time to anticipate his next move or Jami would have been prepared for it—or, better yet, prevented it. But as it was, thought proved to be impossible as Lance Morgan's arms came around her and pulled her to him for a brief but explosive kiss. Jami's hands were pressed against the solid wall of his chest for an instant, her lips teasingly brushed by his and then covered completely by the warmth of his mouth.

Her response was instantaneous and electrifying. A shudder ran through her body, followed by a tingling rush of warmth that actually made her dizzy.

And then it was over. By the time her head had cleared and she had opened her eyes, Lance Morgan was gone.

It rarely happened when the shift was short-handed, but the day proved to be exceptionally slow. The number of calls going out over the air were few and far between, and Jami found herself yearning for the normal hectic pace of a typical weekday. Every time she let down her guard, Lance Morgan's image popped into her head, and it irked her no end.

His behavior had been mercurial, to say the least, and she often found herself thinking of his kiss. Her own behavior was no less comprehensible to her— she had *let* him kiss her, with absolutely no thought of protest. And afterward she felt as if he had some-how branded himself into her being with the searing touch of his lips.

The weather turned gloomy late in the afternoon, less than half an hour before Jami was due to get off duty. Dusk approached rapidly and a steady drizzle fell from a leaden gray sky. Her squad car was stopped

Her gaze darted past him as she absorbed her surroundings. For the first time she noted the sterile white curtain behind him and to her left. Through a narrow opening in the folds, she could see figures hurrying and bustling.

The emergency room. She was in the hospital emergency room.

Her thoughts were still a little disjointed. She remembered receiving a robbery call—and being the first to arrive. No, that wasn't right. She had *almost* arrived . . . .

"An accident," she said slowly as the pieces began to fit together. Her voice sounded weak and strained to her ears, very unlike her usual confident tones. "I was in an accident, wasn't I?"

She looked at Lance for confirmation and he nodded. He watched her intently, his hands resting on the edge of the narrow table she was lying on. She shook her head, hoping to clear away the cobwebs, but the movement caused a pain to shoot through her head and she leaned back against the pillow gratefully.

"How do you feel?"

"My head hurts." She moved it tentatively to look at him, smiling weakly. "If you told me I'd been hit by a steamroller, I wouldn't be at all surprised."

"From what I've heard, you very nearly were," he said. "Try sitting up now so I can take a look at you, but do it slowly."

Jami's eyes widened. "You're going to examine me?"

He arched an eyebrow, a gesture she was beginning to think he reserved solely for her, but his voice was surprisingly mild. "Do you see anyone else around to do it?" When she shook her head, his mouth twitched slightly in amusement. "Looks like you're stuck with me then."

Strangely enough, Jami wasn't resentful. She was feeling a little giddy and light-headed, not at all argumentative. And, she acknowledged to herself, it was rather ironic and maybe even a little bit funny that they had done a radical about-face since this morning's events.

A faint smile touched her lips as she propped herself up on her elbows. "I guess you're going to get your wish after all."

"My wish?"

"Don't you remember? This morning you said you'd like to ply your trade with me. I'll bet you didn't really think you'd get a chance, did you?"

An answering smile hovered on his lips. "No, I didn't," he responded softly. "I wasn't even aware that you'd heard it." There was a brief pause. "In fact, I think I said and did some things I normally wouldn't have."

Like kissing her? Was he regretting it already? A rush of disappointment skittered through her, swiftly suppressed.

"I'd like to apologize."

Jami looked up at him in surprise. "It's all right," she murmured. "I'm sorry, too, for thinking you were a burglar." And for searching you oh-so-thoroughly, a little *too* thoroughly, she added silently, her cheeks burning scarlet at the memory.

"After I had a chance to think about it, I realized there wasn't much else you could have done. I can see where you'd be suspicious," he said. "And if there actually had been someone trying to break in, I'd certainly have been grateful for your presence—but preferably not alone."

His last words slipped right by her. "Does that mean you didn't report me?"

"I didn't report you," he answered softly.

"Thanks," she murmured, relieved at not having to face Sergeant Nelson.

They smiled at each other and Jami felt her heart turn over, both at the warmth in his eyes and at the tenderness of his smile. Lord, she was acting like a lovesick teenager, and there didn't seem to be a thing she could do about it!

The moment was gone, though, when Lance reached for the stethoscope looped around his neck. "Let's have a look at you." His tone was impersonal. "Mind taking off your shirt?"

Jami turned startled eyes upward. "Is that really necessary? The headache is going away and I—"

"In this case, I think *I* know best."

His cool words struck an unwelcome chord in her, and surprise turned to frustration. She glared at him for a long moment before reaching for the buttons at her cuffs. She shrugged off the blue shirt angrily, and, at his nod, yanked off the long-sleeved thermal underwear beneath, tossing them in a pile at her side. She paused for a moment, her eyes mutinous as she looked up to find him presenting her with his broad back.

Lance turned around, his eyes hooded as he looked at her. "This too," he said, flicking a finger toward her bulletproof vest. "And the T-shirt."

Jami reddened at the mention of the T-shirt. She knew what a ridiculous picture she must be presenting to him, peeling off layer after layer of masculine clothing, but wearing a white T-shirt was required by regulation.

Finally she sat huddled on the table, bare from the waist up except for a wispy lace bra that hid little of her porcelain flesh. Still, she was grateful for what little protection it did give her, and was suddenly glad the accident had happened during the winter months. During the summer, wearing a T-shirt and vest under her uniform left her feeling sticky and wilted, and for that reason she usually never wore a bra. The thought of Lance Morgan viewing her body without a stitch on from the waist up . . . well, at the least, the prospect would have left her feeling even more uncomfortable than she already was.

Lance's firm mouth curled slightly as he looked at the small pile of clothing beside her. "No wonder I had trouble picking up a heartbeat. You're wrapped like a mummy."

"It happens to be cold outside," she retorted defensively, "and unlike a lot of people, I don't spend all my working hours inside a nice warm building. Plus, I prefer to have some protection in case I get shot at."

He made no comment. Instead he placed the stethoscope to her chest and listened to her heartbeat for a moment. Then he moved it around to her back. The metal was cold on her bare skin, but Lance's fingers resting lightly on her waist were disturbingly warm.

"Take a deep breath." Jami complied, unaware of the movement of his gaze as it skimmed over her heaving breasts. She felt a slight twinge near her ribs as she drew a breath, but said nothing, since it wasn't all that painful.

"That hurt, didn't it?" Lance asked knowingly as he placed the stethoscope on a small cart behind him.

"A little," she admitted.

"Lie down again for me."

She lowered herself, her eyes on Lance's face as he bent over her. His manner was distinctly business-like and when she found herself wishing for the return of his gentle mood of moments before, she finally admitted the truth to herself. She was attracted to him, *very* attracted to him. When he wasn't snapping at her, she suspected it would be only too easy to like him as well. Too bad she'd never see him again . . . .

Further thought was suspended as Lance's hands glided over her slender rib cage toward her breasts. Though his touch was far from being a caress, it sent a flicker of awareness pulsating through her body, causing her to gasp.

"Is that where it hurts?" he asked immediately, his blue eyes looking directly into hers.

Jami looked away, unable to meet his gaze. She felt confused, unable to cope with her startling reaction to this man. Here he was trying to give her a perfectly legitimate physical examination and she was inter-preting his touch as that of a . . . a lover!

"No," she finally managed. "It's lower, on the left side."

Again his hands probed and touched her midriff, but when the gentle pressure he exerted yielded no more than a slight intake of breath on her part, he withdrew them and turned aside. "That's all," he said briefly. "You can get dressed now."

Jami sat up and reached for her clothing, donning

each piece hurriedly while his back was turned and he scribbled on her chart.

"Nothing broken, right?" she asked when he turned back to her.

"Right," he agreed. "I think you've just been shaken up a bit. How does your head feel now?"

"Not too bad." She put a hand to her forehead and frowned as she encountered a small lump.

"Just a bruise," Lance explained. "You probably bumped your head on the steering wheel."

"I guess that's how I got knocked out," she murmured. Then a thought long overdue occurred to her. "Was anyone else hurt? The other driver . . ."

He shook his head. "You were the only one the ambulance brought in so I'm assuming the other driver was okay."

His eyes met hers and she felt like squirming under his penetrating gaze. "Since you've given me a clean bill of health—"

"Not yet, I haven't." Jami was silent as he examined her further, checking her reflexes and firing questions at her about her past medical history every few seconds.

At last he straightened. "How's your memory?"

"My memory?" Jami drew her slender brows together. "Why?" she asked warily.

"You received a blow to the head serious enough to put you out for nearly half an hour," he said calmly, though something in his tone told her he didn't appreciate her questioning him. "I'm merely trying to rule out any aftereffects."

"Oh," she said in a small voice, realizing how suspicious she'd sounded. She averted her face. "My memory is fine."

"You're sure? No problems remembering what happened last weekend? A month ago? Ten years ago?"

"I'm sure," she said firmly.

"Any nausea or dizziness?"

"None at all. I feel fit as a fiddle." Or almost, she added to herself. Her head was throbbing a little and suddenly all she wanted was tó go home to some peace and quiet. And, a small insistent voice added, to begin the process of trying to forget Lance Morgan, something she hadn't managed the first time around.

A nurse slipped inside the small curtained area to speak with Lance. "You have a visitor," he announced when he turned back.

Jami nodded. "Probably my supervisor."

She was right. A few seconds later, Sergeant Wayne Edwards stepped into the alcove. Jami was surprised to see an expression of concern on his grizzled face as he moved closer. He was hard to please and even harder to like, but despite her personal feelings about him she respected his professional judgment. It suddenly occurred to her that he expected no more of the officers he supervised than he thought they were capable of giving.

"Hi, Sarge," she greeted him.

"Simpson," he acknowledged with a nod of his iron-gray head. "How are you feeling?"

"I won't say I've never felt better, but I'm okay." She cast a quick glance at Lance for confirmation.

Sergeant Edwards turned to him. "That right, Doctor?"

"I think she'll be fine," Lance said. "But she should take it easy for a few days, and she really shouldn't be going back to work today."

Edwards nodded. "Her shift ended at four. so that's no problem. I'll see about having her work the desk tomorrow." He turned back to Jami. "You're off on Friday, aren't you?"

"Yes," she said, trying hard not to grimace. She disliked working the desk, taking incoming phone calls and so forth. It was utterly boring. She much preferred working in the field. Luckily, occasions on which it was necessary to fill in at the desk were rare.

"Any suspects in the robbery call, the one I was en route to?" she asked Edwards.

He chuckled, the action softening his harsh features. "We nailed him almost on the spot. He was in such a hurry to get away and count his money, he didn't bother to watch where he was driving. Guess who caused your accident."

Jami's eyes widened. "You mean the *suspect* is the one who crashed into me?" She shook her head and smiled. "Well, I guess you could say I got my man. Too bad I won't get credit for the arrest."

"Sorry, but there's not much I can do about that," Edwards commented. "You're always on the ball, though. One less arrest isn't going to do you any harm."

Jami blinked unexpectedly. This was the closest she'd ever come to receiving any praise from Sergeant Edwards. It was too bad she'd had to be involved in an accident to hear it, she thought wryly. Another thought suddenly occurred to her. "How bad is the damage to the squad car?"

"It's totaled," he said with a frown. "When Williams and Donner pulled you out, they expected you to be in pretty bad shape. As it was, you scared the hell out of them when they couldn't get you to come around."

"All's well that ends well," she said with a lift of her shoulders. It sounded as if she'd been rather lucky, but she was okay and she wasn't the type to dwell on it.

"You'll need a ride back to the station," Edwards started to say. "Why don't we—"

"That's already been taken care of," a deep voice cut in from behind. Edwards turned in surprise. "Officer Simpson really shouldn't be driving," Lance continued smoothly, "and since she and I are—friends, I thought I'd see her home. Unless there's a problem?" he questioned with a lift of his brows.

"No, no problem. That's fine with me," Edwards said immediately, already on his way out. He glanced back over his shoulder long enough to say, "Glad you're okay, Simpson. See you tomorrow."

He was gone before Jami even had a chance to thank him for coming. She looked at Lance. A suggestion of amusement glimmered in his eyes as he watched her speechless confusion.

"Are you ready?"

Without waiting for an answer, he wrapped a lean arm around her narrow waist and lifted her gently to her feet. A feeling of giddiness swept through her and she clung to his arm until her world had righted itself, then looked up into his tanned features to find concern reflected in his eyes.

"I'm okay," she said unsteadily, releasing him and pushing her arms into the sleeves of the coat he'd placed over her shoulders. "Let's go."

Her mind was riddled with questions as Lance stopped briefly to let the staff know he was leaving and to drop off her chart. He steered her toward the hospital's rear entrance. She didn't understand why

Lance had insisted on taking her home, instinctively knowing it was only going to complicate something she wasn't sure she understood yet.

They stepped out into the chill darkness of night and Lance led the way to a gleaming black Porsche, its lines sleek and graceful under the glare of the street light.

"This is yours?" Jami's eyes widened as she stopped and ran her fingers caressingly over the hood.

"Yes. Do you like it?"

"Oh, yes." Her voice was momentarily trapped in her throat by the smile her response elicited and the unexpected warmth in his eyes.

She nodded and smiled back at him, almost against her will. "Actually, though, I'm partial to the Italian models—Lamborghini, Ferrari . . . I'd give anything to have a Maserati." She laughed, a tinkling sound that was carried away by the moist wind. "I could save my pennies for a dozen lifetimes and still not be able to buy one. Civil servants are notoriously overworked and grossly underpaid."

Lance unlocked her door and helped her inside. After taking his place in the driver's seat, he turned to her. "Why not trade in your badge for something else then?"

"At twenty-six, I'm getting a little old to set my sights in a different direction."

"That's not old," he objected, switching on the ignition. "I was almost thirty before I finished my residency and set up practice."

Jami was silent, tempted for a moment to tell him of her own years in law school. But Lance Morgan was, after all, a stranger, though he hardly seemed like it. And she doubted he would even be interested.

"Anyway," she finished, "this is my first bona fide job other than working on my parents' farm when I was a teenager. And I really do like what I do, despite the fact that it isn't the best paying job in the world. I'm perfectly satisfied being a police officer and driving my little Toyota instead of a Maserati."

Lance glanced at her. "I have the feeling I've just been told to mind my own business," he said dryly.

"I didn't mean to sound defensive." She slipped her hands into the pockets of her coat, waiting for the warmth of the heater to envelope her. "Usually it's the other way around."

"I wonder why."

Jami flushed guiltily as she realized he was probably thinking of the way she had forced him up against the wall at gunpoint. Her own thoughts backtracked to her search, and to his body's involuntary response to her touch.

The car's interior seemed suddenly cramped with his big body only inches away from her own, the size and breadth of him reaching out to entrap her. A sudden and overwhelming desire to escape seized her.

She flashed a sidelong glance at his profile as he stopped for a traffic signal and wet her lips nervously. "Look, Dr. Morgan—"

"Lance."

"All right—Lance." She stopped, surprised at how easily his name fell from her lips. "You really don't have to take me home. If you'll just drop me off at the police station, I'll get my car and—"

"I wasn't kidding when I said you shouldn't be driving. I'm taking you home and that's that."

Jami's lips tightened for a fleeting second before she relented with a sigh. There was something in his tone that convinced her that arguing was pointless, and he was, after all, the one doing the driving.

Chapter Three

Illuminated by the headlights of the Porsche, droplets of water sparkled like tiny diamonds on the graceful branches of the cedar trees at the entrance to Jami's apartment complex. She directed Lance to the spot in the tenant garage where she normally parked her small Toyota.

They had hardly talked at all during the fifteen-minute ride and now Jami turned to him. "Thanks for the ride and . . . everything else too." She hesitated, feeling that her words were inadequate in light of the fact that he'd gone to so much trouble for her, particularly after this morning. After all, he certainly hadn't been obliged to take her home. "Would you like to come in for a cup of coffee?" she found herself offering.

"Sure," he accepted readily, to her surprise.

Lance was right behind her as she unlocked her apartment door. She had the sudden feeling she was being stalked and it made her rather nervous. As a result, she caught her heel and lost her balance when she stepped up to cross the threshold. One booted foot trod forcefully on Lance's instep.

"Ouch!"

"Oh, no! Are you all right?" Jami grabbed his arm and steered him inside her apartment and into a chair as he hopped on one foot.

"Good Lord, woman, and you're supposed to be protecting society? You should be registered as a lethal weapon!"

"I'm sorry," she murmured, watching as he removed his shoe and sock and inspected his foot with a pained expression on his face. Peering over his shoulder, she saw a small bruise already darkening just above his toes.

"If I didn't know better, I'd say it was Friday the thirteenth," she said, only barely managing to stifle a giggle. "This doesn't seem to be a very lucky day for either one of us."

Lance's muttered reply was lost as he wiggled his toes tentatively.

"Do you want some ice?"

"No . . . well, maybe . . . no, I guess not."

"Make up your mind." Jamie paused at the doorway to the kitchen. From the look on Lance's face she'd have thought a truckload of bricks had come tumbling down on his foot instead of her heel! At his continued silence she commented, "If you don't hurry up and tell me, there are going to be *two* invalids in this room. I'm about to wither up and die of hunger."

"Thanks to you, so am I."

Jami couldn't hold back a smile at the sudden, hopeful look in his eye, but all he said was, "Since you obviously don't want to get me any ice, could you at least offer me a Band-Aid?"

"Your foot isn't cut, silly, it's just a little red." Jami was finding out that it was certainly true that doctors and nurses make the worst patients. "Would you like to stay for dinner?" she added.

"Thanks. I was hoping you'd ask."

"I noticed," she said dryly as she made her way into the neat and compact kitchen. She wasn't sure what she'd be able to scrape up since her refrigerator wasn't very well stocked at the moment, but she would make do. She made note of the inventory aloud as she rummaged through the contents. "Let's see . . . milk, eggs, cheese, bacon . . ."

"Sounds like breakfast to me."

She turned to find Lance behind her. "Do you mind? This is the night I normally do my grocery shopping so I'm running low on a lot of things." He had replaced his shoe and sock and was standing a mere breath away. She had to resist the impulse to step aside.

"Beggars can't be choosers," he said, then lifted a lean hand to smooth her cheekbone gently with a slightly rough fingertip. "You look tired. Why don't you go into the living room and rest for a while? If you don't mind me making myself at home in your kitchen, I'll fix dinner."

The gesture was a little too friendly for Jami's peace

of mind, but she was determined not to let him know the disturbing effect his light touch had had on her.

"Breakfast," she corrected in a bantering tone. "And no, I don't mind. In fact, I think I'll take unfair advantage and grab a quick shower while you're slaving over the stove." With that, she left the room, unaware of the sudden frown that creased Lance's forehead as he watched her go.

"Take a couple of aspirin while you're at it," he called after her.

As Jami shed her uniform and cumbersome gunbelt in the privacy of her bedroom, she wondered at her reactions to Lance. There had been a few times this evening when she'd felt completely at ease with him, but the next minute she was acutely aware of his maleness and the way it seemed to wreak instant havoc with her senses. She was far too used to being in control, and it was hard to grasp the fact that she was woefully unable to handle her body's responses to this man.

The shower was a far cry from the long, leisurely bath she really wanted, but it helped restore a measure of her self-confidence. She dressed in a worn but still serviceable pair of jeans and a loose, flowing peasant-style top before taking two aspirin and returning to the kitchen.

The aroma of coffee perking and bacon frying was heavenly, and Jami smiled cheerfully as she entered the room. Lance gave her a quick appraising glance from his place near the stove.

"Good timing," he said, returning her smile as he handed her a plate heaped with food. "Oh, you shouldn't have given me so much," she protested as she sat down at the small round table.

"It wouldn't hurt you to pick up a few pounds." Lance filled another plate and sat down across from her.

"You wouldn't say that if you saw the way I eat." Jami wasn't being modest about her appetite; for a small person, it was huge. She dug into the perfectly cooked omelette with relish. A few bites later she looked over at him, a twinkle in her eye. "You know, I think you missed your calling in life."

"How's that?" Lance asked as he buttered a slice of toast.

"This is really good." She raised her brows appreciatively and gestured at her plate with her fork. "Maybe you should have been a chef instead of a doctor."

"I know one thing for sure." His tone was dry. "I would never have made it as a burglar."

"But you'd make a good car thief," Jami teased, thinking of the relative ease with which he'd maneuvered the coat hanger to unlock her patrol car.

"If the going gets rough, at least I'll have a couple of things to fall back on." He looked at her and smiled, shrugging his broad shoulders. "Anyway, it was either learn how to cook or starve."

His words made it sound as if he'd spent much of his life alone. Had he? she wondered immediately. Before she even had time to think, she blurted out, "Haven't you ever been married?"

For just a moment she read a myriad of emotions in the blue depths of his eyes—surprise, amusement, and, oddly enough, pleasure. Then they were suddenly and totally unreadable. Jami held her breath, waiting almost painfully for his answer as his gaze traveled over the slender arc of her neck and down to the slight swell of rounded breasts hidden under the gauzy material of her blouse.

"No," he said at length, his tone betraying nothing of his inner thoughts. "I've never been married. Until I was thirty, I was too busy working and studying to have much time for anything else."

"And after that?" she asked, hating herself for her curiosity but wanting desperately to know. Perhaps it would give her some clue as to the kind of man he was.

"After that"—he paused and gave her another long searching look that sent her pulses careening madly—"there simply wasn't anyone I cared to see more than a few times." He took a sip of his coffee. "What about you? Any ex-husbands lurking in the background?"

"Nope," she said cheerfully, oddly pleased by his words. "Not a one."

"Ever come close?"

"Never."

"Why not?"

"Same reasons as you, I guess," she said with a shrug, aware of a vague feeling of uneasiness. She was usually the one probing, digging, making judgments. "Besides," she added without really knowing why, "my working schedule is so different from everyone else's. It's a little tricky to get together if a guy asks me out on a Saturday night and I have to work."

"Tricky but not impossible," Lance commented. "Did I hear your sergeant say you were off Friday?"

Jami's heart began to pound. Why was he asking? "Yes," she said in an offhand manner, trying to ignore her quickening pulse. "I have Friday, Saturday, and Sunday off until mid-March."

"Three days?"

She nodded. "We work ten-hour days—four on, three off—and rotate shifts every three months."

The rest of the meal was conducted in a rather pensive silence, broken only by Lance's teasing jibe, "I couldn't help noticing you ate everything on your plate and more. Were you trying to be polite and cater to the chef's ego or were you really that hungry?"

"I was starved," she admitted, smiling a little as she added, "but it really was delicious."

Lance helped her stack the dishes in the dishwasher, but again neither one of them had much to say. By the time the kitchen was restored to its usual spotless condition, Jami's nerves were wearing a little thin.

She straightened the tablecloth for the third time, aware of Lance's eyes boring into her back. What happens next? she wondered a little wildly. Would he go? Would he stay? And what did she want?

One thing was certain—she was far too cognizant of Lance as a man to be very comfortable. She had never felt quite like this before and it left her just a bit wary of him—as well as of herself.

Lance followed her as she finally led the way into the living room, and he glanced around quickly as she switched on a table lamp. The furniture was sleek and modern, but designed more for comfort than looks. An abundance of healthy plants dotted the room, complementing the overall decor.

"This is nice," he said, his eyes lingering on a lush Boston fern perched on a glass stand near the picture window. "I like all the greenery. Plants give off oxygen, you know," he added, a twinkle in his eyes.

"Typical remark, Doctor." Jami laughed, some of

her tension dissolving. His eyes suddenly caught and held hers for a long moment, and she found herself unable to look away, feeling as if she were drowning in murky blue depths.

Lance broke the contact first. "I really should be going. I have an early day tomorrow."

"I'll get your coat," she said quickly. She retrieved it from the closet, trying to avoid his touch as she handed it to him, but he tossed it over the back of a chair. Turning to her, he captured both her hands firmly in his.

"Will you let me kiss you again, Jami Simpson?"

The sound of his voice vibrated huskily in her ears and she took a deep quivering breath. Her flesh tingled where her hands rested in his, and she could smell the clean male scent of him, both sensations combining to make her mind spin crazily. She said the first thing that popped into her head.

"You didn't ask my permission this morning."

Lance laughed softly. "I wasn't on my best behavior this morning."

"Are you now?" The tip of her pink tongue darted out nervously to moisten dry lips, inadvertently drawing his gaze.

"That depends on you," he murmured, eyes lingering on her mouth.

Hardly aware of anything but the warmth of his touch, she looked up at him. The memory of that morning's teasing kiss so vividly invaded her mind and overwhelmed her senses that she felt she was almost reliving the velvety sweetness of his mouth.

Her lips were parted in silent provocation, eyes wide and uncertain as her gaze was drawn helplessly to his. Jami wasn't sure exactly when the touch of his lips was no longer a memory but a reality, a reality she wished would go on for forever. It began as a tentative exploration, his lips closing her eyelids and wandering over the tender curve of her cheek before fully claiming the softness of her mouth.

One hand was transferred to her back, gently urging her body forward. The heated intimacy of Lance's kiss and the feel of his taut, muscled body were a heady combination. Jami's senses awakened, slowly blossoming under the skillful and sensual touch of male mouth and hands. Desire—bubbling just under the surface and waiting eagerly to be released—coursed through her body in shivering waves.

Her hands crept upward over his shoulders and she sifted her fingers through the silky gold hair at the nape of his neck, reveling in the fine texture. Lance gave a low groan and tightened an arm around her pliant body. One hand trailed seductively down her spine, gently probing the slight hollow below her waist before continuing downward. Exerting a subtle pressure with the palm of his hand, he tempted her with the intricate distinctions between male and female, even as he gently propelled her yielding body toward the sofa. His body followed hers as she sank back onto the welcoming cushions.

"I want you," he muttered against her mouth. "Oh, Jami, how I want you . . ."

Warning lights began flashing in Jami's brain. What was she doing? This man was a stranger—she knew nothing about him! She had better put a stop to this now, before things got out of hand—*way* out of hand!

"No." Fighting the treacherous lassitude of her body, she struggled against his heavy weight, despising herself for the weak thread of sound that was her voice. "No," she repeated, more firmly, hands bunched tight against the solid wall of his chest.

She stared up at him as his eyes, dark with passion, finally opened to gaze down at her. "I want you," he said again, the husky tone vibrating through her limbs. She felt an urgent desire to wrap her arms around his neck and draw his head down to hers, to let nature take its course and damn the consequences.

"It won't be a one-night stand, I promise you . . ." His lips discovered the throbbing pulse at the base of her neck.

His words provoked a measure of sanity in her and her hands began clutching frantically at his shoulders. How had she gotten herself into this? Inviting a stranger into her home, sharing a dinner with him, and then letting him . . . Gullible, that's what she was, and the hellish thing about it was that she, more than anyone, knew better than to take people for granted! And as if that weren't enough, the way he made her feel was scary—damn scary!

"No, dammit!" She pushed at his chest with all her might. "I can't . . . I'm not that kind of person . . . I—I don't know anything about you!"

Her desperate cry somehow managed to rip the veil of desire from his eyes. Jami noted with the deepest sense of relief the growing awareness in their blue depths. He raised himself from her body and sat up while Jami scooted back against the arm of the couch, watching as he raked an unsteady hand through his hair.

He turned to her after a few deep breaths. "Look, I'm really sorry—I didn't mean to scare you—"

"You didn't," she snapped, a show of false bravado masking her inner turmoil. She smoothed a fold in her jeans and slowly inhaled. "I think it would be best if you . . ." Her voice trailed off as her gaze lifted to his rugged features. Somehow the words had formed a tight knot in her throat.

"You want me to leave?"

Jami focused her gaze somewhere in the vicinity of her lap and nodded.

"Are you angry?" He rose to stand in front of her. "Upset because I—"

"No," she interjected quickly. After all, it wasn't his fault—at least not entirely. She could have put the brakes on much sooner . . . And *should* have. "No," she said again.

"You're sure?" Firm but gentle hands drew her up.

"I'm sure." Somehow the words weren't quite as resolute as she intended.

"If you're not angry, then prove it."

"Prove it?" Her head shot up in surprise. Dear heaven, surely he wasn't suggesting . . . "How?" she demanded, her head tilted defiantly as she challenged him.

"By thanking me—properly," he said, a distinctly mischievous light in his eyes.

"Thanking you! For what?"

A thoughtful frown creased Lance's brow. "For services rendered?" At Jami's outraged gasp he hastily amended his words. "For *professional* services rendered."

"The Department's insurer will see that you're

paid," she informed him loftily. "That should suffice."

"Well, then . . . for the dinner?" he asked hopefully.

"I provided the food, remember? You only cooked it, so don't you think you should be thanking me instead?" She crossed her arms indignantly, already aware that being even the slightest bit disgruntled with this man was wasted emotion.

"That's a great idea." He moved so close, he was a mere breath away. "We can thank each other."

"Look, we already—" The sound was trapped in her throat as she watched the lights dancing in his eyes fade to something else. He cupped her shoulders in his hands, then trailed his fingertips down her arms. Her body burned with a fierce warmth as liquid fire raced through her veins.

This is wrong, she told herself over and over again. *All wrong.* Lance was going to kiss her again and she was going to let him. Already anticipating the warmth of his mouth, she raised her lips and her eyelids fluttered shut.

But nothing happened.

She opened her eyes, her confused stare focusing on the sensual curve of his mouth.

"I'm not going to kiss you," he said softly in answer to her unspoken question. His eyes caressed the downy softness of her cheek, then moved to her lips. "But I'm not leaving until I get my thank you."

"A proper thank you?" Jami was already rising on tiptoe, hands splayed against his chest for balance, lips hovering for a breathless instant near his. A tremulous sigh lifted her mouth to his and then she was kissing him, wanting desperately to deepen the contact to fervent intimacy but knowing she didn't dare.

When she finally lowered herself to the carpet with Lance's guiding hands at her waist, she was breathless, her pulse racing madly.

"Be sure to call me tonight if you have any nausea or dizziness, or if the headache returns," he murmured into her ear, his breath warm and soft. "I wrote my phone number in the address book by the phone."

"Thoughtful of you." She stepped back and smiled up at him.

"Yes, wasn't it?" He slipped into his jacket. At the door he turned again. "What time shall I pick you up in the morning?"

Jami hesitated, suddenly remembering that she was without a car. "I can call a cab. You don't have to pick me up."

"Yes, I do," Lance corrected. "I want to."

Another chance to see him . . . Did she really want to pass that up?

"Five-thirty," she said softly.

To her delight, he didn't bat an eyelash. A few minutes later she climbed into bed with a half-smile on her lips. The last thing she was conscious of before drifting into sleep was the sweet lingering taste of Lance Morgan's mouth on her own.

Chapter Four

A shrill piercing sound roused Jami from a deep dreamless sleep the next morning. For a long time she lay still, then finally realized the phone was ringing and made a dive for it.

Her first thought was that she'd overslept and Sergeant Edwards was calling to see why she hadn't shown up for briefing. But instead of his gruff tones on the other end of the line, she heard a low, husky chuckle and instinctively relaxed.

"Were you sleeping?" asked a deep velvet voice.

Still half-asleep, Jami sat up slowly and ran her fingers through her tousled dark hair. The memory of last night suddenly rushed into her mind. Her voice husky with sleep and some other emotion, she gripped the receiver more tightly and whispered, "Lance . . ."

"I'm sorry I woke you, but there's something I need to ask you."

"Yes?" Her tone was oddly breathless.

"Will you have dinner with me tonight?"

His directness caught her by surprise and she blinked. She wasn't sure what she'd expected, but it certainly wasn't a dinner invitation. She leaned back against her pillow and smiled.

She glanced at the bedside clock. "You called me at five o'clock in the morning to ask me that?" she reprimanded teasingly.

"Well"—he sounded a little sheepish—"I thought if I caught you early enough, there would be less chance that you'd refuse since you'd be too busy primping and getting ready for work."

The thought of primping for a job where she might end up directing traffic in a steady downpour for several hours or scuffling in the dirt with some heel who didn't want to be taken into custody struck Jami as funny, and she couldn't resist a low chuckle. "I don't primp, Lance."

"Are you always cheerful in the morning or is your good humor reserved solely for me?"

"A little presumptuous, aren't you?" she asked tartly, a bit surprised at how easily the banter sprang from her lips.

"I don't know. Am I?" he inquired lazily.

Good question, she thought to herself, her smile fading as she wondered if he was like so many others she had encountered in her work, always willing to take, but never prepared to give. Yet some deep instinct told her he was considerate and caring.

"No," she said softly, almost thoughtfully. "No, I don't think you are."

"Does that mean you'll have dinner with me?"

"Persistent if not presumptuous," she observed with a soft laugh.

"And you're being evasive," Lance charged lightly, but with a thread of steel underlying the wry humor in his voice.

Jami made no comment, recognizing the truth of his statement. Damn! Why did he have to put her on the spot? Dinner with Lance sounded tempting, maybe too tempting.

"Are you asking me out in exchange for last night's dinner?" she asked cautiously.

There was a sigh on the other end of the line. "That suspicious mind of yours never takes a breather, does it?" Mingled with the dryness in his deep voice was an unmistakable note of censure. "I think you insist on searching for ulterior motives behind even the most innocent remarks." Jami bit her lip as he went on softly. "But to answer your question, I'd like to see you again tonight so we can get to know each other better—for that reason and that reason alone."

She clutched the receiver more tightly, another thought springing into her mind. She had dated a few men who were interested in little more than her body. Was Lance really any different? She had seen people lie, lie with smiles on their faces.

"Jami, I promise I won't touch you, if that's what's bothering you. I know we got started on the wrong foot, and I realize I didn't help matters any last night. I came on a little too strong for you and I apologize." There was a brief pause. "Let's start all over again—tonight. How about it?"

She closed her eyes, not sure if she was disappointed or relieved by his "hands off" rule. Damn, but the man didn't miss a thing! He was too observant, too astute, but most of all—too attractive! How could any woman resist him?

She certainly couldn't. Her next words came out in a rush, surprising even herself.

"I'll have dinner with you tonight."

"Great. I'll pick you up in half an hour and we'll talk about where and when on the way in to work." There was a click and he was gone.

Suddenly eager to begin the day, Jami flung back the blankets and swung both slender legs to the floor, peeling off her flimsy nightgown on the way to the bathroom.

Twenty minutes later she stood in front of the living room window, a steaming mug of coffee in one hand, the other occasionally parting the woven draperies so she could peer outside.

The smooth purr of an engine came to her ears and she peeked through the curtains in time to see Lance's car pulling into the parking area. Dumping the remainder of her coffee into the kitchen sink, she grabbed her gunbelt and dark blue uniform jacket from the dining room table and hurried outside.

"Good morning," she greeted him as she slid into the passenger seat. She sent him a tentative smile before dropping her eyes to her lap as she adjusted the cumbersome gunbelt across her thighs.

"Hi," Lance said easily, blue eyes intent on her profile for a long moment before he put the car into gear and backed neatly out of the small parking space. "Where's your uniform?" he asked, glancing at her beige-colored slacks.

"My uniform?" Jami asked blankly, then laughed nervously. "I do have more than one, you know." She went on to explain. "I always change in the locker room at the Department." She smiled as he lifted a questioning dark brow. "The women's locker room," she added.

They exchanged a subtle look of amusement and Jami found it extremely hard to take her eyes off him. The appeal he held for her was almost mind-boggling. His long muscular legs were covered by dark corduroy slacks and he wore a teak-brown leather coat over his open-necked shirt. How well her fingers remembered the feel of those smooth, supple shoulder muscles . . .

Jami forced herself to focus her gaze straight ahead, but she was still acutely aware of his strong, masculine presence beside her. His clean fresh scent filled the cramped interior of the car and she had to consciously slow her breathing.

"Feeling okay this morning?" he asked with a quick glance in her direction.

"Fine, except when I take a deep breath. My ribs are a little tender." She lifted a hand to her forehead and touched the swollen and yellowish skin under the fluff of bangs. "The bruise on my head looks a little rough, but it doesn't hurt." She looked over at him and smiled. "How's your foot?"

"It would be a lot better if you'd offer to kiss it and make it better."

"No, thanks." She laughed as she wrinkled her nose. "Afraid I'll have to pass on that."

"In that case, it still hurts like hell," he teased.

Jami laughed again and settled back into the plush leather seat, wanting nothing more than to drink in the sight of him but knowing she didn't dare. It was strange, this thoroughly feminine appreciation she had for his hard male body, she who had been enticed by any number of good-looking men without the slightest danger of succumbing. Why did Lance affect her so strongly? She would have to watch herself carefully tonight, *very* carefully. Agreeing to see him had probably been an unwise decision. Could she possibly get out of it?

Apparently their thoughts were on the same wave length. Lance glanced over at her, then said easily, "I thought we might go to Antonio's tonight. Ever been there?"

"No, I haven't," she murmured.

"The food is excellent. I think you'll like it."

Jami bit her lip but made no response. Her mind searched desperately for an excuse to break their date, but her thoughts seemed to be functioning in slow motion.

They were nearing the Civic Center in the downtown area and she directed him to the underground parking garage and into the well where patrol vehicles were kept. There was a locked stairway which led directly up into the Police Department, used only by employees.

She grasped the door handle as he pulled to a halt, then turned to Lance to find him watching her, an enigmatic expression darkening the blue of his eyes. His gaze probed hers until she felt herself weakening, growing warm all over. She knew in that moment that she was lost.

"I'll pick you up at seven." The deep voice cut into her chaotic thoughts. "Sound okay?"

"Sure," Jami mumbled as she got out of the car on rubbery legs and headed toward the stairs.

She took the steps two at a time, fuming inwardly as she gave herself a good tongue-lashing. The dratted man was able to reduce her to a quivering mass of uncertainty; she, Jami Simpson, an independent, self-possessed woman who implicitly trusted her good judgment and instincts. So where was all her self-reliance when she needed it? Where Lance Morgan was concerned, it seemed, she had no will of her own.

Jami took particular pains with her appearance that evening, wearing a camisole silk top of rich burgundy with a matching skirt and sheer overblouse. Her shining black hair was swept up into a soft chignon on the crown of her head.

She flushed with pleasure at the appreciative gaze Lance gave her when he picked her up. "I thought you said you didn't primp," he teased gently.

"Not for work, I don't," she corrected. "This is—different."

"I certainly hope so," he murmured as he ushered her outside and into the night.

Antonio's had opened only recently. Not terribly swank and not terribly expensive, it was a restaurant that had already earned a widespread and well-deserved reputation for its excellent Italian cuisine. Soft light shone from the wall sconces, illuminating the huge room. Shadows of flickering candlelight danced on the rich wood paneling of the walls. It was, Jami decided with pleasure, a restaurant to return to, if only to experience the delight of the old-world atmosphere.

A few minutes after their arrival the waiter came over to their corner table to see if they were ready to order. They both decided on the linguine with red clam sauce. Over the appetizer of crunchy batter-dipped zucchini rounds, the flow of easy conversation took a more personal turn.

"Tell me about yourself," said Lance, his eyes capturing and holding hers. "We never got down to basics the first time around. Or the second," he added, a twinkle in his eyes.

Jami toyed with the stem of her wineglass and smiled at him. "Anything special you want to know?"

He shrugged. "Where you come from, that kind of thing."

"Well, I'm a native Oregonian." She told him of her childhood on the small but self-sufficient farm her parents owned near the central Oregon community of Bend.

"How did you end up in Salem?"

"I attended graduate school here."

"Willamette University?"

She nodded.

"And I'll bet you went to law school."

"Good guess," she confirmed with a smile, "and right on the money."

Lance leaned back slightly in his chair, gazing at her assessingly. "So you're a lawyer turned cop," he murmured.

Jami raised an admonishing eyebrow. "Turned what?"

"Excuse me." He laughed and held up both hands in a gesture of defeat. "I'll correct that—police officer."

"That's better." She chuckled. "But you're not quite right. I never finished law school. I dropped out at the beginning of my third year."

Their linguine arrived and Lance picked up his fork. "How did you become interested in law in the first place?"

Jami hesitated a moment, suddenly a little embarrassed about divulging so much of her life history, but he seemed genuinely interested. "Well," she finally said, "my high school political science teacher seemed to consider me his star pupil, and he encouraged me to give some thought to a related career. I decided I liked the idea and I had visions of becoming the Pacific Northwest's most successful prosecuting attorney. But"—she paused, her smile widening—"it didn't quite turn out that way, as you saw yesterday."

"What made you decide against it?"

"It wasn't so much that I decided against it," she said thoughtfully. "I just found something I liked better."

Lance raised a questioning brow and she went on. "At the time, Salem's Police Department offered a ride-along program to Willamette's law students. One Saturday night when I had nothing better to do, I went along. And after that . . . well, law school just wasn't the same."

Jami was lost in thought for a moment as she went back in time to that memorable night.

Driving through the shadowy streets with a patrolman, listening to the crackle and buzz of the police radio in the darkened interior of the squad car, had sent an odd little shiver racing through her body. And when the officer she was riding with was assigned a call concerning a burglary in progress at a downtown jewelry store, she was thrilled. A silent alarm had sounded when the burglar picked the lock of the building's glass doors, so he had no idea the police had been summoned. She and her patrolman companion, along with several other units, had raced to the scene. They all shut off their flashing red overhead lights and sirens a fair distance away so as not to alert the burglar, then their headlights. The squad cars had rolled up to the curb in total darkness, closing in on the jewelry store and blocking all possible avenues of escape.

Jami had watched from the relative security of the car as four officers surrounded the surprised burglar inside the jewelry store, taking him into custody without so much as a peep.

She'd been scared—there was no denying it—her heart had pounded frantically in her chest, but far surpassing her fear was the exhilaration that surged through her. She found herself wishing she'd been actively involved in the arrest, rather than resigned to the unfulfilling role of passive observer. It was then that she began to suspect that no courtroom setting could ever fill her with such satisfaction and excitement.

Less than a month later she learned the Police Department was in the process of compiling a hiring list for the next year. Without any hesitation whatsoever, she took the written test and the oral exam, doing so well that she placed number two on a list of well over two hundred applicants. Within three months she had accepted a job as a police officer for the city.

At Lance's urging, Jami related the story to him, unaware of the sparkle in her eyes as she spoke. They had finished their meal and Lance seemed relaxed, his elbows on the tabletop, the tips of his long fingers pressed together. An easy smile played at the corners of his mouth and Jami found her eyes drawn to it, fascinated by the sensual fullness of his lower lip.

"I have the feeling you wouldn't trade your job for anything."

She paused, considering, tilting her head to one side. "No, I don't suppose I would," she said slowly, the sparkle in her eyes fading, "although there are . . . certain aspects of the job I could do without."

"Like what?" Lance raised a dark eyebrow.

Jami's eyes darkened and her long spiky lashes dropped to shutter her expression. She sighed, then began speaking in a low tone that hinted at strong emotions held in check. "Like having to tell a father and mother that their only child has just died in a car accident"—that was something she'd had to do only the week before—"or seeing a two-year-old who's been severely beaten by his stepfather, and having some high-and-mighty judge decide he's still better off at home, even though the chances are ten to one he'll be beaten again—even worse than the last time." Her words were bitter and she looked up at Lance to find him watching her with a strangely gentle expression.

"I'm sorry." She attempted a laugh, thinking that he probably had no desire to hear about the more sordid aspects of her job. "I really shouldn't be talking about this—"

"No, go on," he urged. "I like listening to you."

And so she went on telling him about her work. It was strange, but she knew that Lance would understand her feelings of sadness and sympathy for the unhappiness others were forced to endure. Normally she tried to keep her personal and professional life separate, but it was with a sense of relief, almost a sense of purging, that she discussed some of the injustices she had witnessed.

"About a year ago," she recalled with a wan smile, "I got a call from one of the local supermarkets. The manager wanted me to arrest a seventy-six-year-old woman for shoplifting five dollars worth of food." She grimaced. "The only reason the woman took it was because some young punk had stolen her purse and her Social Security check was in it. It happened while she was on her way to the bank."

"Did you arrest her?" he asked.

Jami leaned her chin on her hand and stared into space, not really seeing a restaurant full of people laughing and talking, but picturing instead the old woman's lined and anxious features as they had sat in the store manager's office. The woman had been so scared and all the manager could think about was the bit of money involved!

"No, I didn't arrest her," she said evenly. "I finally managed to talk the manager out of prosecuting, and I paid for the items the woman had taken. Once we were outside, I handed her thirty-two dollars—every cent I had on me at the time. And then"—she looked over at Lance with a pleased but sheepish smile—"I took her to the Social Security office to fill out a claim for the check that had been stolen. From there we went to her bank and she made arrangements to have the check deposited directly into her account. It was all totally unauthorized, but I did it anyway," she added with a slightly defiant tilt to her head.

"I would think the woman would have been fairly appreciative," Lance murmured. "Was she?"

"Oh, yes," Jami said with a laugh. "About a month later she sent me a check at the Department for the money I had given her, and I also got a Christmas card from her this year. Anyway," she concluded, "I guess that incident represents what I like least about my job. What keeps me going is the thought that if I can keep a woman from being raped, a child from being abused, a house from being burglarized, then I've done someone—as well as myself—a service." She paused for a moment, then added softly, "Thank you for listening. I hope I haven't bored you—"

"You haven't, believe me," Lance interrupted, giving her a long, searching look that seemed to stretch into minutes. Jami was on the verge of discomfort when he suddenly covered one of her hands with his own.

"Considering our first encounter I never thought I'd be saying this, but you're a very special person, Jami Simpson." His tone was soft and warm as velvet, yet his words were strangely puzzling. Jami's eyes flew to his face, only to find the corners of his eyes crinkling with a smile.

She dropped her gaze hastily, staring at the tablecloth as if mesmerized. Was he teasing her? she wondered wildly. She had absolutely no idea why he would say such a thing and she wished she could look into his mind and read his thoughts. And his touch! Who would have thought the mere brush of his fingers could provoke such a wild singing response in her blood? Even now she could feel her heart pounding like a pagan drum.

She swallowed hard in an effort to get her mind off her body's treacherous response to him. "What about you?" she asked nervously. "What made you want to be a doctor? Money? Power? Prestige?"

Lance lifted an eyebrow and chuckled. "The same could be said of lawyers, you know."

She let herself banter with him, relieved that the gentle thrust and parry were evaporating her sensual awareness of him. If only it was this easy all the time!

She shrugged. "But I'm not a lawyer," she reminded him, a mixture of triumph and mischief lighting her eyes.

"Got me there," he relented easily, his gaze traveling over her delicate features. "You have to admit, though, that you chose an occupation that is . . . a little unusual for a woman."

Jami arched both slender brows, her full lips tightening for a fleeting second. "The reason it's unusual is obvious," she retorted. "It's only because *men* haven't accepted the idea that women can make a valuable contribution to the profession. As long as a woman is sitting behind a desk and looking pretty, everything is fine and dandy. But put a woman behind the wheel of a squad car and they're singing a different tune!"

How well she knew. She'd had to prove herself twice as competent, twice as dedicated, twice as professional as any of the male rookies who had been hired along with her. The Department's upper echelon had scrutinized her far more closely than her male counterparts before granting her permanent status after her probationary period, despite her coach's constant assurances that she was a good officer. She sat back stiffly, armed to the teeth with ammunition against any comment he might care to make.

But to her surprise, and then embarrassment, Lance's tanned face bore a look of amusement at her show of temper. "You are a bundle of contradictions, you know that? If anyone can keep me on my toes, it's you," he said wryly.

"Contradictory, am I?" she shot back immediately. "Look who's talking!"

Lance shrugged and smiled. "I don't see what you find contradictory about me. As the saying goes, 'what you see is what you get.'"

"That's exactly what I mean!"

"I don't follow you."

"All that blond, sunstreaked hair and those thick dark eyebrows—" She waved a hand in the air and her gaze dropped from his bronzed face to the strong corded column of his neck, then to the opening of his shirt, which revealed a tangle of crisply curling hair, their dark sheen matching that of his brows and forearms. She cut her sentence off abruptly. Part of her wanted desperately to succumb to the urge to indulge herself in an imaginary journey down the rest of that lean male body, sweeping away the barriers of his clothing . . .

Her eyes darted upward to his face as she heard his voice. Luckily he didn't seem to have noticed anything unusual about her sudden silence.

"Oh, that," he was saying with a rich, full laugh. One long brown hand went self-consciously to the back of his head. "Courtesy of an Irish father and a Swedish mother."

Jami seized on his words—anything to get her mind off the havoc he unwittingly created within her body. Her appreciation of his all too evident masculinity was much too thorough, much too sensual, much too . . . just *too much* for her to handle.

"Tell me about your parents," she said breathlessly. "Do you have any other family?"

"My parents died when I was sixteen," he said quietly. "I was an only child."

"I'm sorry," she murmured, silent for a moment. Then she asked softly, "Did that have anything to do with your wanting to practice medicine?"

"No, not really," he replied. "As far back as I can remember, I wanted to be a doctor and I never changed my mind. My parents' death was totally unexpected—a car crash—and they were never really the type to plan for the future."

He spoke of his subsequent years of training—Jami was able to grasp that despite scholarships and grants, money had been a scarce commodity—his days occupied with studies, his nights working at a hospital lab in order to manage living expenses.

She studied him covertly as he talked, noticing not the man in front of her, but the man within—strong, staunch, determined. Yet there was also a gentle sensitivity in his deep voice and a vibrant warmth glimmering in his eyes. An odd thought flashed through her mind. *Here was a man to trust, a man to depend on if the need ever arose.*

Jami was a woman used to using her instincts. *Play it by ear,* the policeman to whom she'd been assigned for training had often told her during her first weeks on the job, *and do what your instinct tells you.* Hah! she thought to herself with a mixture of wry humor and utter wariness. If she did what her heart was urging her to, she'd be wrapped in Lance Morgan's arms this very minute and that would never do!

Completely unbidden, a vision filled her mind, a vision with razor-sharp intensity. She saw herself and Lance, limbs entwined, bodies elegantly bare and deliciously bold, locked in an embrace that only lovers assume . . .

The sound of Lance's voice jerked her back to reality. "Are you all right?" he was saying. "You look a little flushed."

"I'm fine," she said quickly, lacing her fingers together tightly in her lap. She managed to lift her eyes to his face, but found herself unable to hold his gaze for more than a second.

She could feel his blue eyes intent and deliberate on her hot face. She fidgeted nervously in her chair, wishing he would say something, anything. Her own powers of speech seemed to have deserted her for once; her thought processes seemed to be suspended as well.

Finally he glanced at his watch and back to her face. "It's almost ten. You've had a long day and I'm sure you must be ready to drop. I really should be getting you home."

He signaled for the check and a short time later they were on their way to his car. Fortunately, walking into the chill night air restored Jami's normal self-confidence and cleared her senses.

The Porsche quickly covered the miles across town, and before she knew it, they were parked in front of her apartment. Jami opened the car door and turned to Lance.

"Thank you for the dinner. I really enjoyed it," she murmured, a little surprised at the truth of the words. She *had* enjoyed herself, in a way she hadn't thought possible.

He nodded. "I'll see you to the door."

He stood behind her as she unlocked her front door and opened it, leaving it slightly ajar. She had left the outside light on and as she turned to him, the rays illuminated her lovely profile.

Lance's strong features were hidden by a shadow. Jami let her gaze sweep over his tall body, admiring the velvety chocolate-brown blazer and well-tailored slacks molding his lean thighs. A warm confusion trickled up her slender neck.

They stood in silence for a moment, wrapped in a moist breeze. Finally Lance lifted a hand toward her slender shoulder, only to drop it abruptly and jam both hands into his pockets.

Jami suddenly sensed he was feeling just as confused as she was, and smothered the urge to smile. An uncertain and indecisive Lance Morgan was almost laughable; it was such a far cry from the confident, self-assured man she had seen so far.

She wasn't sure she should invite him in, not after last night, and yet she was strangely reluctant to have him leave just yet. "It's hard to believe we got through the entire evening without either one of us having an accident," she finally said.

To her relief, he smiled. "Maybe it's a sign of things to come," he suggested softly.

"I certainly hope so. I don't think either one of us needs a day like yesterday any sooner than the next century."

"It wasn't all bad," he said, his smile fading. "Even though you mistook me for a burglar, I did, after all, meet you."

There was a low, intense note in his voice that sent a wild flurry of excitement skittering through Jami's body. She bit her lip, not sure how to respond. Her eyes sought his in the darkness.

"This doesn't have to end now, you know," he said

gently. "And in all honesty, I don't think either one of us wants it to."

It took a moment for his softly murmured words to sink in, but when they did, Jami sucked in a harsh breath, her uncertainty rapidly giving way to anger as she realized how much of a fool she'd been. She should have known he couldn't be trusted! He clearly thought now was the time to take up where they'd left off last night!

"That's where you're wrong," she bit out in a tight voice, barely able to control her fury at him and her vexation with herself. "If you wanted dessert, you should have ordered it at the restaurant, because I don't intend to—"

"I'm aware of that, Jami. I was hardly asking for bed privileges."

Her eyes flew up to his at the quiet tone. "You—you weren't?"

"No." Lance shook his head, and to her relief she noted a flicker of amusement in his eyes.

Her even white teeth sank into her lower lip, all traces of anger now gone. "Oh, Lance, I'm sorry," she apologized. "I did it again, didn't I?"

"Jumping the gun, you mean?"

"Yes," she said with a shaky laugh.

"I'm beginning to get used to it," he said dryly. As he smiled down at her, his look grew increasingly warm. "I want to see you again," he said in a low, husky tone. "Very much. And I hope you don't mind if I repeat myself, but I think you feel the same."

Somehow his words came as no surprise. Hadn't she felt an inkling of this all along? And he was right—she did want to see him again. So much so, it was almost frightening.

"So what do you think?" There was an oddly shuttered look in his eyes that belied his light tone as he broke into her thoughts. "You think a guy like me and a girl like you . . ."

Jami took a deep breath. "Yes," she said breathlessly, "I think we could."

"Great." Lance touched the tip of her nose with a finger. "I'll call you tomorrow."

He started to turn away, and at the realization that he was leaving, Jami caught at his arm. "Lance . . ." She looked up into his face uncertainly and wet her lips with her tongue. "Aren't you going to . . . kiss me good night?"

His eyes held hers endlessly, his body very still. "Much as I'd like to, I'm not about to push my luck," he said quietly after a long moment. "I made a promise this morning and I don't make promises I can't keep."

He smiled then and Jami felt a rush of warmth in her veins as he said good night and disappeared into the murky darkness.

Chapter Five

The next few weeks went by in a haze, time passing more quickly than ever before in her life. In the past Jami's work had been the central focus of her life, but now she looked forward to her off-duty hours with eager enthusiasm.

And it was because a good deal of that time was spent with Lance.

The demands on his time were much the same as on hers—many and varied—but they managed to spend a considerable number of hours together. And though he didn't stick to his "hands-off" rule precisely, his touch, his kisses, were always featherlight and tantalizing, leaving her with a deep, yearning ache inside.

But Jami wasn't about to quibble—she had already

discovered that her body had a will of its own where he was concerned—and she suspected her mind wasn't lagging very far behind.

The fact that he wasn't pushing made it easier to deal with—certainly it was safer. Call it pride, vanity, whatever—she wasn't the type of woman to jump into bed with a man at the drop of a hat.

The third Friday in January found Jami peering through her living room window, searching for the twin beams of light that signaled the approach of the Porsche. Darkness had fallen an hour earlier and with it had come a bitter chill. The daytime temperature had barely reached thirty degrees, though it was crisp and clear outside. But now Jami could see a group of diamondlike stars to the west being swallowed up by a gloomy cap of storm clouds.

She decided to check her appearance one last time. Darting into her bedroom, she nodded approval to herself in the mirror as she smoothed her black slacks and frilly white silk blouse. Then she heard the soft chime of the doorbell.

Greeting a smiling Lance, she felt as if the air had been suddenly and very forcefully expelled from her lungs. His rugged appeal seemed even more devastating than the last time she'd seen him.

"Hi," she said, forcing a light tone. "You're late."

"I know." His gaze was warm and approving as it swept over her. "I got tied up in Emergency with a heart attack victim."

He told her about the case as they left her apartment and got into his car. Then a companionable silence settled between them as Lance drove toward the heart of the city. But when he turned onto the bridge that spanned the churning waters of the

Willamette River toward gently rolling hills to the west, Jami glanced over at him.

"Where are we going?" she asked curiously. There were few restaurants on this side of the river. The area was mostly residential, much of it farmland outside the city limits.

"I thought we'd go to my place for dinner," he said. There was a brief but significant pause as he glanced over at her, her profile just barely visible in the dim light. "We've seen a lot of each other lately, but you know, we've hardly ever been alone together for an entire evening."

A shiver ran down Jami's spine and she swallowed, feeling as if her heart had suddenly lodged in her throat. He was right—there always had been swarms of people around—and she couldn't help wondering now if it had been intentional on his part. And he'd always delivered her promptly to her door at the end of the evening and left her quickly. *Alone with Lance, totally alone, with no protective buffers. . .*

"Does the idea bother you?" Lance asked softly, stepping on the accelerator.

Jami turned to peer at him in the car's darkened interior. "Being alone with you, you mean?"

"Yes."

"That depends," she said lightly. "Are you carrying me off to your lair to make wild and passionate love to me the whole night through?"

He chuckled. "What do you think?"

Jami smiled. "I think I'm a fool for asking." Lance had been the perfect gentleman thus far. So much so, in fact, that there had been a number of times the last week she'd found herself wishing he were just a little bit more of a rogue.

A few minutes later he turned off the main road onto a narrow winding track that climbed steadily uphill. Jami gave a gasp of delight as he pulled to a halt at the summit.

In front of her was a sprawling contemporary home of rustic cedar, nestled among a smattering of graceful fir trees. Behind her, visible in three directions, were the twinkling lights of the city, spread out below on a blanket of dark velvet.

"This is beautiful," she breathed as she climbed out of the car.

"I'm glad you like it," he said easily, taking her arm. "Come on, let's go in. It's freezing out here."

The interior of the house was just as impressive. Jami fell in love with it on sight. The huge living room contained sleekly styled furniture and a massive stone fireplace dominated the center of the room. The overall effect was of beauty and comfort rolled into one.

"Hungry?" Lance asked, leading her by the hand into an open and airy kitchen done in sparkling white and gold.

"Starved, as usual," she admitted cheerfully. "Anything I can do to help?"

An hour later they sat down at the small butcher-block table to what seemed like a feast to Jami, since she'd skipped lunch. An easy camaraderie flowed between them as they ate the broiled steaks, fresh fruit salad, baked potatoes, and tender young asparagus spears topped with a tangy cheese sauce.

Stuffed almost to the point of bursting, Jami pushed her plate away and shook her head. "I'll say it again, Lance. You should have been a chef. Everything was fantastic."

Lance speared the last bite of steak with his fork. "You deserve some of the credit too." His eyes skimmed over her slim figure and one corner of his mouth went up. "You constantly amaze me. I don't see how such a small woman can put away so much food."

"Hollow legs," she assured him with a poker face, then grinned. "And I get plenty of exercise chasing after some of our fair city's not-so-upstanding citzens."

After making quick work of the dishes, they returned to the living room. Jami sank down on the sofa and leaned her head back, letting her eyelids close as her body relaxed.

It was strange, she mused, how much at home she suddenly felt. It seemed almost as if she had lived here always, known Lance always . . .

The sound of his voice drifted into her reverie. She turned her head to the side and smiled at him across the small space that separated them. "I'm sorry, I didn't hear you."

"I just said"—he leaned toward her slightly and slid his arm along the back of the couch—"looking at you now, it's hard to believe you're a cop. I might be able to see it if you were six inches taller and fifty pounds heavier, but as it is . . ." He shook his head as if he were very puzzled indeed.

Jami's smile faded. His words struck a note of displeasure deep within her, immediately bringing to mind a hulking, not particularly feminine, woman.

"The fact that I'm a police officer," she said tightly, emphasizing the last two words, "doesn't make me any less a woman."

The bite in her tone was unmistakable. Lance's

eyes flickered a little in surprise. "Who are you trying to convince?" he murmured. "Me? Or yourself?"

"I'm not trying to convince either one of us," she shot back. "I just don't appreciate being criticized for no reason at all."

"I wasn't being critical." He frowned a little as he withdrew his arm. "Merely observant."

Jami's small chin lifted and her eyes narrowed as she looked at him, a nagging feeling tugging at her. There was something right in front of her nose here. What? Suddenly she recalled his words the night they'd dined at Antonio's. *You have to admit, though, that you chose an occupation that is . . . a little unusual for a woman.* And then it clicked. Why hadn't she seen it before?

She faced him indignantly. "You don't approve, do you?" she demanded.

"Approve? Of what?"

"Of the fact that I—a woman—am a police officer!"

Lance stared at her and Jami had the feeling they were squaring off to do battle. His tone was quiet but faintly challenging when he finally spoke.

"Frankly, I don't."

Jami's eyes blazed furiously. "What is it you don't like?" she asked archly. "The fact that I'm a woman doing a so-called *man's* job, and doing it just as well? Or do you simply dislike the idea of female police?"

"Now wait just a minute—"

Jami jumped to her feet, continuing as if she hadn't even heard him. "Do you also disapprove of female doctors? Female engineers? Female executives?" Her laughter held no mirth and her accusing gaze never left Lance's taut features. "Funny, you really had me fooled! You've never even bothered to let on how you felt about my work, when all this time you've been silently disapproving. I certainly never thought you were a male chauvinist!"

Lance was beginning to get a little angry himself. "If you will sit down and control yourself for a minute, I'll try to explain."

His tone was sharp and Jami suddenly realized she'd gone a little overboard—maybe. But if there was anything that triggered her temper, it was men who felt there was no place for a woman in police work except behind a desk. And she couldn't help feeling hurt . . . yes, *hurt*, that Lance hadn't cared enough to make his feelings known right from the start.

"Go ahead and try," she said stiffly, sitting down again but refusing to look at him. Her mouth was a thin straight line in her pale face and two bright spots of pink stood out on her high cheekbones.

"All right then," he began firmly. "I don't think the fact that I can't necessarily agree with your career choice has all that much to do with *us*. I am interested in Jami Simpson, the person, not Officer Jami Simpson. Did you really expect me to bring up something that we obviously don't see in the same light?" His jaw hardened. "We were just getting started, and you were suspicious enough without adding fuel to the fire. Put yourself in my place for once. Can you blame me for avoiding the issue?"

Her anger slowly dwindled and a sigh escaped her lips. It all sounded so logical when Lance explained it.

"I guess not," she murmured, glancing at him. "And I'm cautious, not suspicious." She sighed again. "Anyway, you still haven't told me what you have against policewomen."

"It's not a matter of having anything against

them." He smiled wryly and some of the tension drained from his face. "I have absolutely no qualms about women in professional jobs, as long as they're qualified." He hesitated, watching her closely. "I simply feel that in the case of policework, there are undoubtedly instances in which a man would be better suited for the job."

"Undoubtedly," she echoed dryly, sending him a smug look. She had a very good idea of what he was getting at. "Would you care to name one?"

"Well." He rubbed his chin, eyes thoughtful. "During a knock-down-drag-out fight between a couple of big bruisers, for instance." His eyes made a leisurely tour of her—from her head to her toes—sending a flood of warmth through her veins. But she determinedly ignored it. "You can't tell me you'd be much good in a situation like that," he said carefully.

Jami turned steady amber eyes his way. "I not only can, I will. It's been my experience that on occasions like that, having a woman around happens to be a definite asset."

Lance raised a skeptical brow.

"It's true," she insisted. "A lot of men are less likely to strike a woman than they are another man. They seem to view a woman's presence less resentfully and intrusively, despite the uniform."

"That might be true in a few cases—"

"I've seen it happen, Lance. Quite a number of times."

"Then you've been damn lucky!" he snorted.

"Maybe. Maybe not." She smiled to herself. He could be right, but so far the worst injury she'd suffered while on duty was a bite on the forefinger while trying to handcuff an escaped female prisoner who still had escape on the brain! At any rate, she had an idea.

"I think," she announced as she rose gracefully to her feet, "I may be able to set your mind at ease."

"How?" His tone was skeptical as he watched her walk to the middle of the room.

"Come here and I'll show you," she said, taunting him with a soft laugh. Lance Morgan was in for the surprise of his life! Her eyes sparkled as she waited for him to unfold his rangy body from the sofa.

"Wait a minute," she said when he was standing in front of her. "I wouldn't want you to get hurt on anything." She glanced at him through a thick fringe of lashes as she pushed the heavy oak coffee table and several other pieces of furniture out of the way. Finally she straightened up and flashed him a dazzling smile. "Ready?"

"I suppose you want me to tackle you or something like that," he said grimly, a scowl darkening his features as he looked down at her.

"Something like that."

"Come on, Jami. You can't be serious!"

"Oh, but I am." She smiled, clearly enjoying herself.

"For heaven's sake, you're a hell of a lot smaller than I am. I could hurt you!"

"Five feet four, one hundred and three pounds," she said sweetly.

"See what I mean!" he exploded. "I've got nearly eighty pounds on you!"

"You won't hurt me," she said, lifting both hands and beckoning to him. "Now come on. Rush me."

Lance expelled his breath slowly and shook his head in sheer disbelief before making what was clearly a reluctant decision. "Just remember one thing," he grumbled, "I'm an internist, not an orthopedist. If you get hurt, don't come crying to me for sympathy or anything else!"

With that, he lumbered slowly toward her. When he was almost on her, Jami grabbed his upper arms, straightened her flexed knees, and expertly twisted her right hip upward, all in one fluid motion.

The next instant Lance was flat on his back at her feet, a look of utter amazement in his eyes. With a grunt he levered himself to his feet, his look now distinctly wary.

"How the hell did you do that?"

Jami laughed delightedly at his reaction. "Trade secret. Let's try it again, only this time put some muscle into it. I'm not made of glass, you know."

This time he did put more effort into it, but again he found himself in a heap at Jami's feet—as he did again and yet again.

"One last time," she invited, beginning to puff a little. She wasn't about to let Lance in on it, but her back was starting to hurt. He was heavy!

"You're really enjoying this, aren't you, you little sadist," he growled as he lifted himself from the carpet.

"Let's just say I'm having in-service training a month early."

Jami was actually a little rusty in her defensive maneuvers, but she put everything she had into this last throw. As a result, Lance hit the floor with a pronounced thud, landing heavily on his back in a tangle of long legs and flailing arms.

When he didn't get up right away, Jami looked down at him more carefully. One arm was thrown to the side and his long dark lashes lay in a heavy crescent on his cheekbones. A sudden flicker of fear went through her.

"Lance?" she called with a frown, then more urgently, "Lance, get up!"

He still hadn't moved so much as a muscle and Jami dropped to the floor anxiously, suddenly afraid he had hit his head when he landed. *And all because I had to prove he was wrong and I was right!* she thought wildly.

Now wait a minute, Simpson, she told herself, taking a deep, steadying breath. Don't panic here. Swallowing convulsively, she placed a trembling hand on his neck to feel for his pulse. It was there, slow, strong, and steady beneath her fingertips. When she shook him again and he still didn't respond, she rocked back on her heels, deciding it was time to call for an ambulance. If Lance had some kind of head injury, there was nothing she could do for him.

The next instant she found herself lying full length on top of Lance, hands twisted behind her back and legs securely pinned beneath his.

A soft gasp flew from her lips and she stared down at him, unable to say a word. He seemed to be the only person on earth able to render her speechless.

"Caught you off guard, didn't I?" He grinned up at her, triumph lighting his eyes. He was clearly pleased with himself.

"Off guard!" she sputtered after a second. "You tricked me! I really thought you were hurt . . . you . . ." —she tried to think of a fitting name for him and came up blank—". . . oh, you medicine man!" she finished lamely. "Let me up!"

"Not yet," he said smugly. "I think I like having the upper hand with you."

"Upper! More like lower!"

The words had no sooner left her mouth than Jami found their positions reversed. She drew in a startled breath, her glance flashing up to his face, then lingering on the strands of gold which fell carelessly onto his tanned forehead. He looked rugged and handsome and boyish, all at the same time, but above all, so damned virile it took her breath away!

The length of his body covered her own completely, hard and compelling and undeniably male. She suddenly knew she had to break this disturbing contact with him before things got out of hand. Speech was again impossible and she squirmed vainly to free herself from the cumbersome weight above her.

Lance watched her struggle, at first with amusement, then with some other emotion. His eyes darkened to sapphire.

"Jami."

The quiet word stopped her movements and her eyes locked with his.

"If you don't stop squirming, I won't be responsible for what happens next. Our first meeting should have taught you that I'm a man, not a eunuch, or hadn't you noticed?"

"I . . . noticed," she echoed faintly. Afraid to probe too deeply, suddenly afraid of the desire she might find reflected in his eyes, she focused her gaze on the collar of his shirt. "Lance, please," she whispered, "you're crushing me."

He shifted to the side immediately, but propped himself on his elbow in such a way that she still couldn't move without some part of her coming into contact with his hard body. And somehow she suspected that wouldn't be at all wise.

Lance's other hand rested lightly on her hip for a moment. Then it moved slowly, possessively, up her slender rib cage and across the thin silk until it stopped mere centimeters away from the downward slope of her breast.

Jami's heart beat crazily in her chest and her mouth was dry with . . . what? Fear? Anticipation? Or was it both?

"You're right about one thing." His whisper was low and husky, threaded with just a hint of laughter. "You're certainly not made of glass." His voice lowered by subtle degrees. "No hard, sharp, cutting angles . . . nothing but smooth, soft, feminine curves."

She moistened her lips with the tip of her tongue, an unconsciously provocative gesture. "Please Lance, don't . . ."

"Don't what?" The huskiness lingered, but there was a vibrant urgency to his low tone. "Don't say such things? Don't touch you? Don't want you . . ."

His voice trailed off as his head descended toward hers. Jami stared up at him wide-eyed as his lips brushed hers slowly and evocatively. Her eyes fluttered closed and with a helpless moan she reached up to tangle her small hands in his hair, wordlessly urging him to claim her mouth completely.

His kiss was both tender and hungry, his tongue creeping into her mouth to explore the warm receptive caverns within, sending a wild swirling into the pit of her stomach. Her response to the intimate crush of his body was explosive, and she found herself glorying in it, every cell in her body awash with searing pleasure. Nothing, absolutely nothing on earth could have made her pull away from the envel oping cloak of his arms. The realization both fascinated and overwhelmed her.

Hardly aware of what she was doing, Jami slid her hands down his back, reveling in the feel of the solid muscled contours beneath her fingertips. Easing back ever so slightly, she brought her hands around to the front of his shirt, exploring with equal delight the flat hard planes of his chest. As she moved her hands slowly downward, then up again, she could feel the slight raspiness of curling chest hairs under the thin fabric of his shirt. A sudden urge to feel the heat of his flesh consumed her. She trembled slightly as she undid the buttons of his shirt, inching unsteady fingers inside the opening and tentatively raking through the thick mat of wiry curls covering his chest and taut abdomen.

Through the pleasure-filled haze surrounding her, Jami felt rather than heard the low groan of pleasure from his throat mingling with her own warm breath. Lance moved his hand over the swell of her breasts in a tantalizing motion, eliciting a firm and excited response from the soft pink crests. Jami felt as if bolts of lightning were shooting through her veins at the gently teasing caress, then gasped as he let his hands slide to the gentle outcurve of her hips.

Time seemed to stand still. The embrace continued for long, endless moments, and yet Jami felt bereft when Lance gently lifted his mouth from hers. He kissed her eyelids open and ran a finger down her small uptilted nose.

"Now that wasn't so bad, was it?" he asked lightly.

Jami smiled slowly. "I'm not sure." She sighed playfully, her arms still looped around his neck, reluctant to let him go. "Maybe we should try it again."

His firm mouth curved upward. "You'd better think twice before you issue an invitation like that. I might be tempted to take you up on it."

"Such indecision," she mocked softly, loving the way his blond hair fell across his forehead, reveling in the intimate pressure of his lean body against her own softness, but missing the moist warmth of his mouth. "If you can't make up your mind, I'll just have to do it for you."

Wasting no time in suiting action to words, she pulled his head down, her mouth instinctively seeking his. His lips parted hers in a soul-reaching message, conveying pleasure and delight at her offering. Jami was just starting to lose herself completely when, seemingly from far away, she heard a harsh beeping. As if to escape the noise, she tightened her hold on Lance, but he was already pulling away from her.

"Oh, God, Jami," he groaned, burying his face in her neck. "It's the hospital. I've got to call. An emergency . . ."

Jami eased away from him, releasing him, her passion ebbing quickly in the face of duty. She avoided looking at him as he stood and crossed the room to the phone. She sat up slowly, lifting a shaky hand toward her loosely coiled topknot, which was threatening to spill down over her shoulders.

After adjusting the pins in her hair, she got to her feet, casting a covert glance at Lance as he stood near the end table, engrossed in his phone conversation. She saw a frown etch its way between his straight dark brows and wondered how he could appear so calm, so composed, as if the passionate exchange between them had never happened. Even now, his nearness was disarming, the mere sight of his strong male body nearly as potent in its effect on her as it had been a few short moments ago.

Lance hung up the receiver and turned to her. "Something has come up and I'm needed at the hospital right away." He paused, adding what was obviously an afterthought. "Want to come with me?"

Jami shook her head quickly. "No, I—I think I'll stay here, if you don't mind. I wouldn't want to get in anyone's way." Not only that, but she desperately needed some time alone to compose herself, to conquer the feeling of weakness which still pervaded her limbs. She thought of asking him to take her home, but dismissed it when she remembered he'd said it was an emergency.

"Sure you won't change your mind?" he asked, and she nodded. He strode to the closet and retrieved his leather jacket, slipping it over his broad shoulders. "I shouldn't be gone long. Don't be afraid to make yourself at home."

Chapter Six

The house seemed terribly empty after he left. Jami returned the furniture to its former position, and then, after several minutes of wondering what to do with herself, she spotted some magazines in a stand near the fireplace. Sitting down on the hearth, she flipped through a few, not at all surprised by what she found. There were current events and sports magazines, but she settled for one featuring the year's newest sports car models.

Ironically enough, the magazine fell open to a page displaying a beautiful flame-red Maserati. Instead of admiring the car's sleek low-slung lines, she found herself remembering the night of her accident, when she'd confessed her desire to own one of the expensive Italian cars.

The thought brought a fleeting smile to her lips. At the time she had certainly never dreamed that a few weeks later, she'd be rather snugly ensconced in Lance's home for the evening—and sharing more than just a meal.

Replacing the magazine, she headed toward the stairway she'd seen off the entrance hall. Downstairs, she found what she was looking for in a huge recreation room off the garage—a television set—and she spent the next hour idly watching comedy shows.

Finally, with a discontented sigh, she switched off the set and decided to make a quick tour of the rest of the house. The upper level was really all that was left, so she headed there, hoping Lance wouldn't mind her curiosity.

There were three bedrooms and a small study upstairs, and Jami found herself lingering in the last room she'd chosen to explore.

The color scheme was indigo blue and taupe, a change from the warm browns and earthy rusts in the rest of the house. The furniture was heavy oak, the lines smooth and simple. It was a beautiful bedroom, and she knew it was Lance's.

Jami looked around the quiet room. She could sense him, almost feel his presence. Even if she hadn't recognized the dark knit sweater folded over the back of a chair or smelled the familiar scent of his cologne lingering in the air, she'd have known.

A movement behind her caught her attention and she whirled around to find Lance stepping into the room. He halted, his jacket suspended by a finger over his shoulder and his other hand resting against one lean hip. A slow smile spread across his face.

"When I told you to make yourself at home, I certainly wasn't expecting to find you *here* when I returned." He was obviously amused. "But then, I guess I should have expected it."

Her eyes widened at this. She was a little disturbed by his words. "Why?"

Lance shrugged, his smile deepening. "Nose of a cop and all that," he offered in explanation.

Jami relaxed, a reluctant smile tugging at her lips. "Once a cop, always a cop," she quipped, and they both laughed. "Actually, I got bored and I really didn't think you'd mind if I took a look around."

"Of course not," he said softly. His eyes bored into hers intently, something flickering in the clear depths. A faint feeling of uneasiness crept into Jami's limbs and she glanced at her watch.

"It's almost midnight," she said quickly. "Would you mind taking me home now?"

An empty silence followed, increasing her apprehension. Why was he shaking his head? she wondered a little wildly, not daring to speculate. And why was he staring at her like that? He looked almost regretful and yet . . . determined.

"Lance?"

He took a step toward her and again shook his head. "I'm sorry, Jami. I can't do that."

"You can't take me home?" Had she really heard him right?

"I can't take you home tonight," he repeated. His eyes met hers, his expression unreadable. "I'm afraid you'll be spending the night here."

Spending the night! Her eyes narrowed abruptly as she flushed with anger. Who did he think he was— and who did he think he was dealing with here? A spineless ninny who didn't know up from down, who she was or where she wanted to go? A quiet dinner . . . just the two of them . . . dammit, was it all part of a little seduction scene? And how dare he assume that she would follow blindly where he led?

"Thanks for asking"—she lifted her chin and sent him a caustic look—"but I think I'd rather spend the night in my own bed—alone."

She tried to march past him, but he caught her arm. The touch of his fingers burned through the thin silk, causing her heart to race at a merciless pace. But it was hardly a pleasant feeling as it had been so many other times.

The next instant she felt herself propelled toward the window. Lance thrust aside the draperies. "What do you see out there?"

His tone was unexpectedly rough and Jami's gaze flew upward to the rigidly carved lines of his face before it turned to the window. She stared into the damp blackness of the night. "I—I don't see anything." What was she supposed to see, for heaven's sake? She was beginning to think Lance was going off the deep end, but a quick glance at his face convinced her to look further. She peered outside more intently. "It's raining a little—"

"*Freezing* rain," he broke in harshly. "The roads are covered with black ice."

Black ice! So that was why he wanted her to stay here tonight! Lord, and she had thought . . . "I could always call a cab . . ." she began without thinking.

"The sanding crews aren't even out yet. For God's sake, Jami"—his voice held exasperation tinged with disgust—"you, more than anyone, should realize the hazards of driving on ice. The only reason I didn't stay in town tonight was because you were here. I was damn lucky to make it home." He stopped and inhaled harshly, clearly having trouble keeping a lid on his temper. "You're staying here tonight and I won't take no for an answer!"

Jami knew that her impulsive words warranted an apology. She had immediately jumped to the conclusion that his reasons for insisting she stay with him were purely physical, purely selfish, motivated by only one thing—sex! But when she glimpsed his tightly clenched jaw, she realized he wasn't in any mood to accept an apology, and while he was in this mood she wasn't particularly disposed to make one.

"All right, I'll stay," she said tersely. "Where should I sleep?"

"Down the hall," he said impatiently, striding across the room, pulling a shirt from a drawer, and thrusting it into her hands.

Jami followed him silently as he marched ahead of her, a little irritated at his behavior. She'd agreed to spend the night—no more questions asked—so what was his problem?

He switched on the overhead light and motioned her inside one of the guest rooms. Jami advanced across the floor a few steps, but noted none of the furnishings. All her attention was riveted on Lance's cold and angry features, the coiled tension in his body as he leaned indolently against the doorframe, arms folded across his chest. The blue iciness of his gaze made her shiver. He looked dangerous and unpredictable.

"Thank you." Her tone was quietly subdued. She wished he would stop staring at her. It was positively unnerving.

The words had barely left her mouth when Lance

straightened abruptly. "There's no lock," he said in a silky tone. "Try not to strain your back while you're moving the furniture against the door."

Jami's mouth tightened. "Come off it, Lance! I wouldn't do that and you know it!"

"Really?" He lifted a skeptical eyebrow, his tone mocking. "Forgive me for saying so, but coming from you that's a little hard to believe."

"Hard to believe!" she echoed sharply. "Of course it isn't!"

Lance laughed, a brittle sound that stiffened Jami's spine. "What's wrong?" he asked harshly. "Don't you like being the object of someone else's suspicions?"

Her eyes narrowed. "So that's what this is about. You're upset because I . . . because you . . ." She stopped. Lance was right—she didn't like having the tables turned.

"Go on," he invited, a hard light in his eyes. "Say it. Because you thought . . . ?"

Jami squared her shoulders. "Because I thought you were going to try to make love to me," she said clearly, "and because I thought that was the only reason you brought me here in the first place." She lifted her chin and met his gaze levelly. "Look, I'll admit I was wrong. Now if you don't mind, I'm tired and I'd like to go to bed—"

"But I do mind," he interrupted in that same silky tone. "I'll leave you alone, but not before you tell me something. You *like* the way things are between us, don't you?"

She eyed him warily as he took a menacing step closer, his mouth a grim slash in his face. "I'm not sure I know what you mean."

"I think you do." His eyes narrowed. "No demands, no obligations. Everything cool and easy and simple. It's a change from your professional commitments and you like it that way," he said again.

Jami bit her lip. This interrogation was making her extremely uncomfortable.

"I'm still waiting."

His tone was grim and she realized she wasn't going to get out of this without getting singed a little. But what could she say? She could hardly get wet if she didn't take the plunge and there was certainly something to be said for gauging the depth of the water before diving in. It *was* easier this way—her emotions weren't so involved that she couldn't make a rational decision where Lance was concerned—that happened sometimes. And yet . . .

She met his gaze levelly. "I'll be honest, Lance. It has its advantages, as well as its disadvantages."

"I see," he said slowly, his lip curling slightly. "Typical of you, Jami. Very typical."

Jami felt herself prickling like a cat at the sharpness of his tone. "Playing at being a psychiatrist, Lance?" she asked tauntingly. "It's not your area of expertise, remember?"

"It doesn't take a psychiatrist to know what your problem is," he told her evenly, eyes intent on her face.

"So now I'm a basket case?" Fuming, Jami sat down in the room's only chair and crossed her legs leisurely. "What's the diagnosis, Doctor? Don't pull any punches—give it to me straight."

"Stop being flip," he said grimly, his long legs carrying him to the spot directly in front of her. "This isn't funny."

"I never said it was." Her eyes glittered as her lips turned up in a saccharine smile. "So what's my problem? Or maybe I should be more interested in the cure?"

"You never quit, do you?" A strong pair of arms shot out and hauled her to her feet. "You want it straight? I'll give it to you straight." His face was an iron mask of grim determination as he stared into her startled eyes. "You just can't forget you're a cop. You're as suspicious *off* the job as you are on it. Sometimes I think you look at everything through a haze of doubt, digging for motives that aren't there, searching for shadowy figures in broad daylight."

Jami gasped at this blatant attack, speechless with shock for a moment—but only for a moment. "Stop it, Lance," she ordered. "You have no right—"

"No right?" His fingers bit into her shoulders punishingly. "How can you say that?" There was a burning glitter in his eyes as he said fiercely, "Dammit, I care about you! If I didn't, I sure as hell wouldn't have adopted the guise of a saint these last few weeks. Believe me, I learned very quickly that one mistake with you was one too many, so I kept my distance, hoping you'd learn to have a little faith in me. But I'm beginning to think a perfect angel would be hard put to earn your trust!"

Jami gaped at him, her mind in a whirl, only one thought finding its way through the jumble. "You—care about me?" If he did, he had a funny way of showing it, snapping her head off as if he couldn't stand her!

"Of course I do," he said impatiently. "If you hadn't been so damn busy cross-examining me every other minute, you'd have known it a long time ago." He swore viciously. "And to think I actually thought you were beginning to . . ." He closed his eyes as if in pain.

She stared up at him. He cared about her . . . how much? How much did he care? "What do you want from me, Lance?" she asked suddenly.

He opened his eyes and looked down at her pale face, her clear golden eyes, now wide and troubled. Some of the harshness left his features. There was a seemingly endless silence before he said heavily, "Maybe more than you can give." He shook his head. "Remember the old woman you told me about, the shoplifter you gave the money to?" She nodded. "Sometimes I think that was a fluke, completely out of character for you. You don't trust anyone, do you?" At her slight hesitation, he continued grimly, "I only know I'm getting a little tired of these trips to the witness stand."

The witness stand . . . Had she really done that? A weary blackness seemed to grip her soul. Lance was a doctor, people relied on him, trusted his judgment, looked to him for advice. It was a fact of life in his profession.

She met his eyes unflinchingly. "Absolute trust?" she asked quietly. "Blind faith? Is that what you want?" She shook her head wearily. "You're right, I can't forget I'm a cop. It's a twenty-four-hour-a-day job, just like yours. Crime doesn't clock out when I do. One life is all I've got, one chance is all I've got. I can't afford to look at the world through rose-colored glasses."

"Maybe you can't change and maybe you shouldn't." His hands dropped from her shoulders. "You don't do things halfway, Jami. Everything is cut-and-dried with you. You see things strictly in terms of black and white, high and low, good and bad. I'm on the offensive and you're on the defensive. No one can make it alone, but you? You're determined to try. It's you against the world."

Lance lifted a hand toward her, only to let it fall limply to his side. For the first time Jami noted the grooves carved so deeply into his lean cheeks. "So where does that leave us, Jami?" he asked quietly, sounding as if he had the weight of the world on his shoulders. "Where does that leave us?"

He turned and left the room.

An hour later Jami was still tossing and turning in her bed, unable to sleep. Jagged words and half-formed phrases chased through her mind. Lance had exaggerated . . . hadn't he? Or was she really as—her mind balked at forming the word—as *paranoid* as he'd made her out to be?

Finally she rolled onto her back and tucked her slender arms behind her head, staring up at the eerie shadows dancing on the ceiling.

Suspicious—how many times had Lance teasingly called her that? Quite a few. Only she had always preferred to think of it as being cautious.

But there was a world of difference, as she was just beginning to see. She was always trying to second-guess him, to delve beneath the surface. Tell it like it is, Simpson, she admonished herself sternly. Jumping to conclusions was a far more accurate way of putting it. Yes, that summed up their relationship very nicely, at least her end of it. And all in the name of caution.

Why? She wasn't sure. In all that she did—her job,

her home life—there was that ever-present element of caution. Perhaps it was instinctive, or maybe a habit. Yet somehow it was no shock to realize that Lance was very important to her and that tonight was in all likelihood the turning point in their relationship.

Where does that leave us? he'd asked. On opposite sides of the road, that's where. And one thing was suddenly crystal clear. As it stood right now, they were going nowhere . . . *fast.*

Determinedly she pushed the blankets aside and swung her legs over the side of the bed. Lance was right, she didn't do things halfway. And this was going to be all or nothing . . .

Outside the wind blew fiercely through the giant fir trees, whipping the stately branches, and an occasional volley of ice slapped against the windows. Jami peered into Lance's bedroom, scanning the darkness, barely able to make out the dim outline of his motionless form in the bed.

He sat up abruptly as the door was gently pushed open. Jami's slender figure was silhouetted on the threshold.

"What is it, Jami?"

Her heart plummeted to her feet at his harsh tone. He was still angry with her!

"I need to talk to you." To her relief, her voice was clear and steady.

A deep silence followed this announcement, a silence punctuated only by his harsh intake of breath.

"Yes?"

Jami's insides quivered at his impassive tone, but she forced her unsteady legs to carry her across the room toward Lance, the light from the hallway spot-lighting her path to his bed. She halted a few feet away from him.

Her gaze swept over his naked torso, lingering on the thick mat of hair that covered his chest and stomach before disappearing beneath the blanket loosely drawn up to his waist.

Her eyes jerked upward to his face and she found him watching her with a knowing gleam in his eyes. Flushing, she pressed damp palms against his shirt where it skimmed the tops of her bare thighs. This wasn't going to be easy.

"I want to apologize, Lance. I judged you too quickly, as well as unfairly, a number of times. But I'm especially sorry about tonight. I've been very suspicious of you all along without really knowing it, and I've had absolutely no reason to be." She faltered for a second before plodding ahead in a low voice. "I . . . I suppose it was a defense mechanism that I . . . I thought I needed. I guess I just overreacted."

Her mouth dry, she waited for his reaction, with a crazy mixture of hope and fear. Her nails dug into her palms so hard, she thought they might bleed.

"Come here."

She obeyed the quiet command numbly, her feet carrying her to his bedside without her knowing it. She wished desperately that she could see his expression, but his face was hidden by shadows.

Lance's hands were warm and strong as he pulled her rigid body down beside him. Jami sat stiffly, not knowing what to expect, wishing this unbearable waiting was over. Her long feathery lashes drooped to shield her eyes from the probing intensity of his gaze.

"It wasn't easy for you to come to me, was it?"

Lance retained his grip on her hand, his fingers idly toying with hers. Jami forced herself to ignore the disturbing contact, but his touch was oddly comforting.

"It was easier to do that than it was for me to realize what I've been doing all this time," she admitted.

"So you came in here to give yourself to me?"

"Yes," she said breathlessly. "If—if that's what you want."

"I don't want sex from you, Jami," he said quietly. "When two people care about each other—really care—there's no giving, no taking, only sharing." He lifted a hand and gently turned her face to his. She had no choice but to meet his eyes. "Since it's confession time, do you mind if I have my say?"

Half-afraid of what she would see, Jami looked deeply into his eyes. Her heart nearly melted at the warmth she discovered there, and she felt as if a life sentence of imprisonment had just been lifted. She shook her head quickly. "Lance, you don't have to—"

Strong, tender fingers were laid against her lips. "I do," he corrected. He dropped his eyes for a moment and seemed to hesitate. "I was pretty rough on you," he said with a shake of his head. "I didn't mean to be. You have to believe that."

"Lance, I know why you were angry . . ."

"Frustrated, not angry. I saw everything I'd been working for just floating away from me and there wasn't a damn thing I could do about it." He lifted her hand to his lips and kissed her fingers slowly, leisurely, one by one. "Can you find it in your heart to forgive my outburst?"

"You only did what needed to be done to make me

open my eyes," she said breathlessly, delighting in the feel of his lips on her skin.

"That doesn't answer my question."

"Does it really matter now?" She smiled at him tentatively, savoring this new closeness between them.

"Hell, yes, it matters," he growled, frowning. "Now tell me, woman."

Jami felt a sudden rush of tenderness for him, along with a tingle of excitement at his last words.

"Yes, you're forgiven," she said softly.

Lance caught his breath at the captivating picture she made—the dazzling brightness of a smile meant for him alone and the mass of long raven tresses tumbling over her shoulders in unconscious sensuality. His eyes were drawn to hers, and suddenly they were caught fast in a visual embrace so intense that Jami felt as if their souls were slowly blending together.

Their gazes locked endlessly, the air between them fraught with sexual tension as each became attuned to the excitement only the other could provoke.

"Do you want me, Jami?"

"Yes . . . oh, yes." His quiet, direct question was as unexpected as her own whispered response was uninhibited. She closed her eyes slowly, giving both mind and body free rein over her emotions. How she wanted him, wanted him in the most basic and primeval way possible. Though he was no longer touching her, she felt consumed by him—by his nearness, by the warmth generating from his naked, hair-roughened skin, by his clean male scent. She slowly drew a deep quivering breath.

Lance shifted his body forward. He slipped a hand under the silken fall of her hair, cradling the nape of her neck. His thumb traced a delicious path along the sensitive column before his fingers slid through the long fragrant strands.

"I love your hair," he whispered huskily, delighting in the silky texture against his fingertips. "I've never seen it like this before. It's beautiful."

For an instant he stared deeply into her eyes, then his head bent with almost agonizing slowness toward the parted softness of her mouth.

A tremor coursed through Jami's body at the light touch of his warm mouth. Totally of their own volition, her arms crept up to circle his neck. Lance's gentle, undemanding kiss was a healing balm, the only medicine her wounded soul needed to erase the bitter words that had passed between them.

His hands framed her face and he planted searing kisses on her nose, her eyelids, trekking across the downy curve of her cheek to the rapidly accelerated pulse throbbing at the base of her throat.

"I want to see you," he muttered hoarsely against her neck. "All of you."

His arms tightened convulsively for a second, then he lifted his head and drew back from her slightly. Jami's eyes, heavy-lidded with pleasure, fluttered open to encounter blue eyes ablaze with passion. A wave of heat suffused her entire body at the knowledge that she and she alone had kindled this fire in him.

His gentle hands moved up her narrow rib cage and Jami became aware of the tantalizing touch of his fingers, the faint brush of his knuckles against her heated skin as he deftly unfastened the buttons which hid the secrets of her body from his gaze.

Looking deeply into her eyes, he muttered hoarsely, "Please, don't stop me! I want to look at you . . . I have to!" He released his breath in a warm rush of air that caused her to tremble.

Trapped in a net of fiercely rising desire, Jami's gaze remained riveted on Lance's face as he pushed the shirt off her shoulders. It fell in a heap around her slender hips and was pushed aside by his hand.

Jami's need to feel desired was almost painful and her breath rattled unevenly in her throat. She sat motionless as a statue as he drank in the sight of her pale flesh shimmering in the opalescent light, his gaze lingering for a never-ending moment on the high, firm thrust of her breasts.

"Beautiful," he whispered. "Absolutely beautiful."

Her nipples tingled in response to both his words and his searing gaze, but she suddenly ached for the feel of his hands on her body, needing the reassurance only his touch could give.

"Lance, please," she whispered brokenly, lifting her eyes to his in silent entreaty.

But he made no move to touch her. Instead he searched her eyes with soul-wrenching intensity.

"Will you sleep with me tonight?"

Jami's eyes dilated with shock, her mind racing along with the drumbeat of her heart. It was a test—she knew that. But if she refused, she could lose all that she had gained these last few moments. And if she did sleep with him . . . She trembled with indecision. It wasn't easy to wipe the slate clean and start over. But hadn't she known that?

Jami found and Lance received the answer in the same moment. It was as if some force beyond them was controlling their actions. Lance's strong arms circled her waist at the same instant that Jami leaned against his hard body. They were fused together—satin-smooth softness melting into bronzed muscle and sinew—in a contact so incredibly sensual, she shuddered with delight.

Lance lay back, taking her with him as he turned on his side and faced her, kicking aside the covers. He wore only a brief pair of shorts, and Jami found herself wishing he were completely nude as she had guessed he might be. The urge to see every inch of his taut male body nearly overwhelmed her.

But such thoughts were cut short as Lance made her quiveringly aware of the other needs of her body, as well as of the pure pleasure a man can give a woman. His hands followed the path his gaze had traveled earlier, paying sweet homage to the gently burgeoning fullness of her breasts. He brushed his thumbs slowly across each throbbing peak, then replaced them with the moist warmth of his mouth.

Such exquisite sensations . . . pleasure and delight beyond anything she had ever known. The erotic touch of his mouth on her soft breasts triggered an uncontrollable desire to know the full extent of the delights his hands and mouth could evoke.

Lance's breathing was ragged as he lifted his head to gaze at her, his need for her an endless reflection in his eyes. "Oh, Jami, do you know how much I've longed to touch you like this? It seems like forever . . ." His voice was rough with emotion.

"I—I thought you didn't want sex from me," she said, gasping, unaware of how illogical her words were in light of her own mounting desires. Lance pressed gentle, teasing kisses upward along the slender column of her neck, yet she sensed there was suddenly something different in his touch. She couldn't seem to think straight. What was it?

"Sweetheart," he growled into her ear, "if you don't know the difference between this and sex, it will be my pleasure to show you."

A relieved sigh escaped her lips. Her body was clamoring for the relief only he could give and she closed her eyes and waited breathlessly for him to renew his passionate discovery of her willing body.

The seconds ticked by slowly.

Finally she opened her eyes to find him staring down at her with a grin.

"Wh-what are you waiting for?" she whispered uncomprehendingly, and then the truth hit her like a truckload of bricks. Lance wasn't going to make love to her!

Stunned, she looked at him, blinking back hot tears. He had deliberately set out to arouse her, to stoke and kindle the fire of her desire, only to douse it completely long before the ultimate moment of fulfillment. Why? *Why?*

She had to know. All sign of passion left her body. In its wake was a wealth of disbelief and incredulity. "I don't understand . . ." she began unsteadily.

"Then I'll explain," he said swiftly, his smile fading as he saw the overbright shimmer of her beautiful eyes and the tremulous set of her mouth.

"No matter how much I *want* to"—Lance reached out and molded her slim hips to his own, causing Jami's eyes to widen at the implicit evidence of his passion for her—"I couldn't, in good conscience, make love to you tonight."

An incredibly tender hand stroked the trembling line of her jaw, but Jami still didn't understand, refusing to look at him until he lifted her chin with a forefinger, forcing her eyes to his.

"I want it to be perfect with us," he said quietly but firmly. "When it happens, I want it to be as natural as life itself. I don't want either of us to feel we have to prove something to the other." He hesitated. "And if we made love now, I'd never be sure of that after what I said to you earlier." There was a brief pause. "Do you understand?"

Yes . . . yes, she did understand, she thought in dawning wonder. Lance didn't want her to feel obligated to make love simply because she had made the choice to continue their relationship, but in a new and different direction—a choice he felt he had compelled her to make. A surge of emotion welled up in her heart for this man who valued her feelings as much as he did his own.

A gentle smile flitted across her face and she turned to him, a teasing light in her eyes. "You really meant it *literally* when you asked me to sleep with you tonight, didn't you?"

An expression of relief crossed Lance's face before he responded lightly, "Can I help it if you jumped the gun again?"

"I didn't see you trying to set me straight!" Eyes glowing with wicked laughter, Jami moved so that the upper half of her body was against his chest. "I think you deserve some of your own medicine." And she proceeded to torment his mouth with her own until he groaned aloud with sheer pleasure.

She lifted her head triumphantly, reveling in the warm glow of his eyes as they caressed her face. But it seemed Lance was determined to have the last word. "Better be careful or you'll get your wish, through no fault of my own," he taunted with a laugh that told her it wouldn't take a great deal of persuasion on her part to push for that to happen.

"Well"—she smiled down at him—"I'm going to see to it that you get yours. Turn off the hall light so I can get some sleep, will you?" With that, she rolled off him, turned her back, and pulled the blankets over her body, unable to recall ever feeling happier.

Lance turned off the light and returned to the bedroom.

"Woman," he growled into Jami's ear as he climbed into bed, pulling her soft body back against his own and curling his legs around her rounded bottom, "I have the feeling you're going to drive me crazy."

Chapter Seven

Pale gold light filtering through the drapes roused Jami the next morning. Memories flitted into her brain, memories of a night spent wrapped in the warmth of a pair of strong male arms, memories of the slow and steady beat of Lance's heart under her ear as her head lay on his solid chest. She burrowed more deeply into the mattress and hugged her pillow, slowly becoming aware that the warmth that had surrounded her throughout the night was gone.

Suddenly the blankets were yanked from her shoulders and a sharp slap strategically placed on her derriere.

Jami turned over with a gasp. Struggling to a sitting position, she grabbed for the sheet and pulled it up over her bare breasts, glaring at Lance.

"What did you do that for?"

Lance's eyes flickered over the gentle swell of silken flesh straining against the thin sheet, and he watched the agitated rise and fall of her breasts with blatant masculine appraisal.

"Jealousy," he replied softly. "Sheer jealousy."

"Oh?" Slender dark eyebrows arched skeptically. "Of what?"

"The way you were holding that pillow. I'd much rather it was me."

"Well, if you were aiming for the pillow, you landed a little short of the mark," she said, smoothing the tangles in her hair with her free hand.

Lance strode quickly to the bed, and her eyes were drawn irresistibly to the muscled expanse of his chest above dark corduroy pants belted around his narrow hips.

He sat down next to her, his weight nearly wrenching the sheet from her grasp. Jami latched onto the ends frantically, suddenly acutely aware that she was naked except for her brief lacy panties. Her eyes darted around the room for the shirt he had loaned her the night before. It was nowhere in sight.

"The shower is all yours." One lean finger trailed across the satin-smooth skin of her bare shoulder, then his gaze lowered to the pulse that had begun racing wildly at his casual touch. "If you need a back scrubber . . ." He let the sentence trail off meaningfully, lifting both dark brows inquisitively.

"Thanks, but no thanks," she said firmly, determined to keep a lid on her emotions. "I've managed for twenty-six years without one, so don't hold your breath."

"There's a first time for everything." He shrugged.

"Besides, I thought a daredevil lady cop like you would be willing to try anything once."

"Then you thought wrong," she retorted. An all too familiar languor was beginning to steal through her body at his extreme closeness. She could see the individual curling hairs on his chest, see the tiny, glistening droplets of water that still clung to the thick matting, smell the clean aroma of freshly soaped skin mingled with his own male scent. Lord, at this rate she'd be taking him up on his challenge in no time at all!

A nice hot shower sounded heavenly, but she wasn't about to give him a free show by parading nearly nude into the bathroom, a good twenty feet from the bed. Last night he had caressed her with his eyes, as well as his hands and his mouth. It almost seemed like a dream to her now, but this—this was only too real.

"Lance"—she shifted uncomfortably—"I'd really like to take that shower, if you don't mind."

He extended a hand toward the bathroom door. "Be my guest."

Jami fumed silently at the innocent look on his face. He was very well aware that she wanted him to leave the room. "It might be nice if I had a little privacy," she informed him, only managing partially to keep the sting out of her tone.

"For you, maybe—not for me," came the glib reply.

"Oh, come on!" Jami was thoroughly exasperated by now. "The naked female body is certainly nothing new to you. You must see dozens every day."

"Hardly," he responded, a teasing glint in his eyes. "All I see are bits and pieces of both men and women from eight to eighty. And besides, when I'm at the office, it's what's inside that concerns me more than what's outside. Unless, of course, *you* happen to be the patient," he added with an infuriating half-smile.

Jami's lips tightened firmly. This whole exchange was showing signs of rapidly turning into a battle of wills and she was determined not to be on the losing end. Squaring her bare shoulders, she looked him straight in the eye. "I'm not getting out of this bed until you leave the room."

"You may be here all day then. Care for some company?"

"You have a comeback for everything," she muttered under her breath, wishing she could wipe that smug grin off his face with a snappy retort of her own. But before she could even think of one, her stomach rumbled loudly.

Jami bit her lip in embarrassment. Then, seeing the flare of humor in Lance's blue eyes, her vexation with him vanished and she couldn't hold back a sheepish smile.

"I think," Lance said dryly as he rose from the bed and took a gold-colored pullover sweater from the dresser, "I'd better leave so you can have your shower and then indulge that voracious appetite of yours. Hunger does strange things to people, or so I'm told."

When she was sure he was a safe distance down the hall, she sprinted for the bathroom. Inside the bronze-tiled room she looked around with appreciation, a pleased smile softening her expression as she spotted her clothes folded neatly on the long vanity.

Half an hour later, feeling revived and refreshed despite the need for a change of clothing, Jami found Lance seated at the kitchen table.

"Coffee's over there." He nodded toward an automatic coffeemaker on the countertop before burying his head in the newspaper once again. "Help yourself."

After filling a mug, she seated herself across from him and reached for a doughnut from the plate in the center of the table. She nibbled it, enjoying the unexpected warmth of the sun's rays beating down on her back through the kitchen window. It was hard to believe after last night's ice storm, but the sky was a clear shade of azure, without a cloud to mar its beauty. Typical of the Pacific Northwest, she thought. One minute it was raining, the next, the sun's golden rays were transforming the glistening droplets of moisture into a dazzling display of colors arching across the sky.

She had just finished her second doughnut when Lance folded the paper and pushed it toward her with a grin and an appreciative look.

Jami flipped her hair back over her shoulder as she opened the paper to the front page. She had worn her hair loose and flowing today, unable to find the heart to wind it into its usual topknot after Lance's compliment the night before.

"Well, well," she murmured, tossing a teasing glance in his direction. "I was beginning to think you'd forgotten you had a houseguest."

Lance ran a finger down to the end of her nose. "Forget you? Never," he vowed with a smile.

A strange sense of complacency warmed Jami's body in spite of her earlier brief moments of doubt. It felt so right to be sitting here with Lance, sharing his breakfast, his coffee, his newspaper—in fact, it felt as natural as waking up in his bed.

She bent her head and pretended to be absorbed in

reading. Matching his bantering tone exactly, she said, "You're wasting your time if you're trying to flatter me. I'm immune."

"You think so?"

"I do," she said with a twitch of her lips, finding it hard not to succumb to the buoyant feeling inside her.

Lance chuckled heartily. "I know something you're not immune to."

"You think so?" She echoed his phrase.

"I know so."

What happened next, Jami was never sure. One minute she was smug and secure in her own chair, the next, she found herself snugly ensconced on Lance's lap. A pair of lean muscular thighs were under hers and powerful arms formed a tight band around her body.

Her eyes were wide with surprise as she struggled vainly to free herself. "Lance, let me go! What are you—"

"Shhh! There's a point to be proven here," he informed her, not hesitating in the least to begin his demonstration.

Firm lips took possession of hers in a kiss of such devastating intensity that Jami became a trembling mass of longing, a willing victim of his passion. Her mouth blossomed under his, opening to him as she felt his breath mingle with her own, warm and sweet and satisfying beyond belief.

With obvious reluctance Lance finally released her mouth, one hand urging her head onto his shoulder before it slipped under her blouse to stroke the smooth skin of her lower back.

Jami smiled as she let her fingers trace the firm contours of his lips, lips that could bring her pleasure in a way she had never dreamed existed. When Lance touched her, it was as if . . . as if she were being given a glimpse of heaven.

"I have to admit," she relented softly, "I think you might be right. There are a few things about you I'm not immune to."

He pressed a kiss into her palm, then lifted her hand and settled it on his thigh, covering it with his own.

"Jami"—his low voice had a husky edge to it that thrilled her down to her toes—"would you like to spend the weekend at the beach?"

"The beach?" She lifted her head from his shoulder and stared at him.

"Yes. I have a small house there, north of Newport. I was just thinking . . . I'm not on call anymore this weekend, and since the weather seems to be halfway decent here, maybe it would be nice there too."

"Would we be spending the night there?" Despite her most stringent efforts to keep her voice on an even keel, there was a slight tremor to it. She awaited his answer tensely, half-afraid to hear a "yes" and half-afraid to hear a "no."

"I thought we might," he said quietly, his eyes intent upon her face.

A momentary confusion assailed her and she felt as if she were being fired upon at point-blank range. Last night she had been ready and willing to share everything with Lance, but she had been caught up in the throes of passion. Now, in the cold light of day, the choice had to be made again. A calm, rational decision was called for, but a decision that called into play her senses, her emotions, her very being. She closed her eyes and prayed, prayed that her choice would be the right one.

His fingers were running lightly up and down her lower spine, intent on smoothing away the sudden tension in her body. "You don't have to sleep with me, Jami. There are two bedrooms."

She flushed guiltily at his words, detecting a faint note of censure in his tone. But a quick glance at his face revealed nothing but forbearance.

She chewed her lower lip uncertainly and looked deep into the vivid blue depths of his eyes. The memory of last evening's scene in her room suddenly vaulted into her thoughts.

Absolute trust. Blind faith. How could she . . . She caught herself just in time, just before she made a fool of herself again. The night spent in Lance's arms and in his bed had proved beyond a doubt that he was worthy of her trust.

Who was she trying to kid? She *did* trust him.

The eyes she lifted to his were bright and full of spirit. "I'd love to spend the weekend there," she said simply.

A gentle hug indicated his pleasure. Then he lifted her off his lap and onto her feet. "I'll tell you what," he said, "I'll let you drive my car on the way over if you promise not to break any speed laws. It's not a Maserati, but—"

"It's probably as close as I'll ever come to driving one," she finished with a grin. "In that case, what are we waiting for?"

It was another hour before they were finally on their way. Lance packed a small bag for himself and took Jami back to her apartment. She hastily changed into jeans, a velour top, and a lined jacket, then threw a few things into an overnight case.

If a twinge of apprehension occasionally bothered her, it was swiftly pushed aside. As the miles sped by, Jami felt as if she'd been given a new lease on life. There was an easy companionship and warm intimacy between her and Lance that was better than anything that had been there before. Sounds of laughter and carefree banter filled the interior of the small car.

Jami guided the car through the gently rolling hills along the coastline. Flanking the highway was a lush green forest of fir, hemlock, and spruce. She drove with deftness and precision, enjoying the smooth purr of the engine and the harnessed power under the hood, which she controlled with sure movements of her hands on the steering wheel or a subtle depression of the accelerator.

They were more than halfway to their destination when Lance turned in his seat to face her, a rather serious expression darkening his eyes. "Do you ever think about returning to law school?"

"I haven't for a long time." She sent him a quick glance. "Why should I? For the most part, I like what I do."

"I think you'd make a damn good attorney."

Jami blinked a little at his quick response and at the conviction in his voice. Remembering the repercussions of their discussion on the subject the night before, however, she decided to keep the tone light. "For all you know," she chided with a smile, "I might have been flunking out."

"Not you," he said, shaking his head. "Unless I'm very wrong, once you make up your mind to do something, you do it. You can be very single-minded when you want to. No half-measures for you, right?" He paused, and she could feel his gaze boring into her.

She shifted a little in her seat, pretending to concentrate on maneuvering around a sharp curve. Somehow she sensed that his words weren't exactly a compliment. Finally she forced a laugh and said, "I get the idea I didn't succeed in convincing you that policewomen are just as capable as men." She wasn't angry, nor was she surprised that Lance hadn't been convinced by either her arguments or her demonstration last night. She had already found out that the firm set of his jaw reflected a very determined side of his character. Or maybe stubborn, she thought with a wry smile.

Jami glanced at Lance and saw a rather sheepish expression on his face. He caught her look and they both laughed.

"I still think I can convince you," she said smugly. "There was a study done in Canada recently." She went on to quote from that study and from several others that had concluded women were as effective as men in the law enforcement field. She cited numerous incidents that had involved either herself or the other women officers on the force that she felt bolstered her case.

"Well," she said with a toss of her head when she'd finished, "have I made a believer out of you yet?"

Lance raised his brows. "I have just one thing to say. You argued a damn good case!"

"Then I *did* convince you," she announced, smiling triumphantly.

Lance held up a hand and laughed. "Let me finish. I

was going to say that I still think your talents are
wasted."

A sigh escaped her lips and she admitted to a small
pang of disappointment. "Well, at least I tried."

"You haven't lost yet, Jami." A half-smile played at
the corners of his mouth as he turned to look at her.
"Let's just say the jury is still out."

At least he was leaving the door open, she thought,
relieved. And it really wasn't all that important, at
least not right now. She didn't want their difference
of opinion to drive them apart, and with that thought
she dismissed the subject from her mind.

A short time later they were headed south on Highway 101. Since it was past noon, they stopped briefly
at one of the fresh seafood markets along the road for
a shrimp cocktail. At Jami's prompting, Lance took
over the driving so she could enjoy the scenery. However, she found most of her attention focused on the
man to her left rather than on the rugged coastline to
her right. The appeal of his chiseled features was irre-
sistible.

When Lance slowed the car to pass through the
small waterfront town of Depoe Bay, Jami insisted he
pull over into one of the many parking spaces along
the highway. There were dozens available during the
winter months, but at the height of the tourist season the tiny town's sidewalks were crammed with
people visiting the numerous gift shops and tourist
attractions. It was often necessary to drive up one of
the steep side streets to find a place to park.

"Pull over here!" she cried. "Please!"

Lance threw her a puzzled glance but did as she
requested.

"Come on!" The car had barely rolled to a stop when

she was out on the sidewalk, impatiently waiting for Lance to join her.

"I suppose we're going to have to spend the afternoon exploring every single one of those souvenir shops," he growled indulgently as he grasped her elbow. "Women and their shopping sprees!"

Jami wrinkled her nose at him. "Even you, I wouldn't subject to that horror." She pulled up the collar of her fur-lined jacket and smiled at him. "No, I have something else in mind."

"Care to let me in on it?" he asked as they walked briskly toward the tiny rockbound harbor.

"Sure. There's a place up here that charters deep-sea fishing—"

"You want to go deep-sea fishing?"

"No, silly! But last summer when a friend and I were driving through, I noticed that the same place offered a short cruise—half an hour or so—on the ocean." She paused for breath. "I've never been in anything bigger than a rowboat, and ever since I saw the sign, I've wanted to try it. So I thought, as long as we're here . . ." Her voice drifted off and she looked up at him hopefully.

Lance could no more resist the entreaty in those beautiful golden eyes than he could deny the depth of feeling she aroused in his body. He nodded ahead toward a tiny building just above the mouth of the harbor. "Is that the place?"

Jami followed his gaze, her eyes darkening when she saw the strips of plywood nailed above the counter. "Oh, darn," she muttered, coming to an abrupt halt. "It's closed."

"For the season, I imagine."

"I didn't think about that." She sighed. "Oh, well, maybe I'll get another chance this summer."

Lance was about to agree when he felt a tap on his shoulder. Turning, he saw a man wearing the rough woolen clothing of a fisherman, his lined face tough as leather from years of exposure to wind and sun.

The man cleared his throat and gave Lance a toothless, apologetic smile. "Didn't mean to eavesdrop, but if the lady's interested in a quick run, I might be able to help."

"Do you own a boat?" Jami asked excitedly before Lance could say a word.

The man shoved his weatherbeaten cap up higher and grinned at her. "No, ma'am, not anymore. But a friend of mine does." He turned and pointed to a small red fishing vessel docked in the harbor. Jami could see a bright scarlet cap bobbing up and down on the deck. "That's Al Peterson. I'll bet he wouldn't mind doing you a favor. He just put in a new engine and I know he's planning on taking the *Misty Rose* out for a trial run any time now. We can find out if you want."

"Oh, Lance, could we?" Jami turned to him, her eyes glowing with excitement.

"Well . . ." At first he seemed skeptical, but at the look in her eyes he relented. "All right, we'll see if he's willing."

The old man led the way down the steep wooden stairway to the docks below, Lance and Jami trailing behind. After introductions and handshakes all around, it turned out the vessel's captain was only too willing to take on a couple of short-term passengers. When Lance offered to reimburse him for his trouble, he steadfastly refused.

In fact, Al Peterson looked pleased as punch when the vessel chugged out of the harbor. They passed a Coast Guard cutter in the process, and all three on board were unable to hold back a laugh at the disbelieving expressions on the faces of the cutter's crew members, who craned their necks to peer at the couple huddled on the deck, only their heads sticking out from a bright yellow tarp tied around them to shield them from the brisk wind.

Lance turned his head toward Jami, breathing in the soft sweet fragrance of her hair, but his nose wrinkled wryly as another, more pungent odor wafted toward them.

"I hope you know"—he bent his head toward her so the captain wouldn't overhear—"we're both going to need another shower after this."

Jami smiled up at him happily, more than content to have his sturdy body so near her own. "I guess the accommodations aren't the best." Her gaze shifted to the thick coils of rope, yards and yards of fish net, and a dozen or so crab pots that surrounded them. "But admit it—this is fun!"

"I can think of other things I'd rather be doing that might be more . . . fun."

The undertone in his voice left Jami with no doubt as to his meaning, and it quickly earned him a strategically placed jab in the ribs.

"It's a good thing you're sitting down," she said huffily, pretending to be affronted, "or I might have put an end to your idea of 'fun' for good."

Lance rolled his eyes upward and groaned. "I keep forgetting you're a woman who knows how to defend herself against a man."

"Next time don't forget it," she told him teasingly,

and turned her attention to the sea. A forceful gust of wind permeated the thick tarp and Jami shivered despite the warmth of her jacket. A strong arm tightened around her shoulder and she burrowed further into Lance's body, flashing him a grateful smile.

The salty tang of the sea air was invigorating. Jami watched delightedly as the dancing crests of the waves rose and fell in tune to nature's rhythm. They were several miles from shore when her stomach lurched unexpectedly and her head swam dizzily. She took a deep breath, telling herself it was only a response to an unusually high swell.

But the feeling grew more intense over the next few minutes and finally she had no choice but to acknowledge that she was seasick!

She swallowed the rising feeling of nausea in her throat and touched Lance's arm. "Lance?" Her voice sounded weak and drained, nothing at all like her own. "Would you please ask Mr. Peterson to turn around? I—I'm not feeling well."

Lance glanced down sharply, noticing that her body was limp and sagging against his. He immediately knew what was wrong. For a moment he was sorely tempted to laugh. Jami had been so gung ho about this idea in the first place and now it really seemed to have backfired.

But seeing the sickly pallor of her skin, he wasted no time in removing the tarp and striding toward the captain to make his request.

By now the uneasy feeling had spread throughout Jami's body and sweat broke out on her forehead despite the chill air. She closed her eyes and wrapped her arms around her stomach in an effort to ward off the waves of nausea, but nothing seemed to help. The murmur of voices came to her as if from a great distance, and she was aware of the boat veering into a sweeping arc as they changed directions.

The trip back to the harbor seemed to take forever. By the time they docked, Jami couldn't even hold her head up. She tried to murmur an apology to Lance and Al Peterson, but all that came out was an unintelligible mumble. Hardly ever sick, Jami was more miserable than she'd ever been in her life.

Lance picked her up and strode to the car, holding her limp body firmly in his arms. Though it couldn't have been more than twenty minutes before they arrived at his coastal home, it seemed an eternity to Jami. And it certainly didn't help matters when Lance had to stop the car several times along the way while she lost her lunch.

Her mind vaguely registered an A-frame, rustic-looking house set on a bluff above a rocky stretch of beach before Lance once again swept her up in his arms. He carried her inside, climbed a winding staircase, and deposited her gently on a king-sized bed.

"God, I feel awful," Jami mumbled into the softness of a down pillow. "How long is this going to last?"

"A while, from the look of things." She heard his deep voice above her head.

He began stripping away her clothing and dropping it in a pile on the floor. Feeling as she did, Jami offered no protest, not even when he slipped her completely nude body between the sheets. Her lashes drooped on her pale ivory cheeks as she snuggled into the mattress, but even all this comfort did little to halt the tumultuous upheaval inside her body.

"Oh, Lance," she groaned, forcing her lids open. He was sitting beside her, smoothing wispy tendrils from her temple. "Isn't there anything that will help?"

He hesitated for a moment. "There is," he said slowly. "But first you have to tell me something. Are you pregnant?"

Chapter Eight

"Pregnant?" Jami repeated in a dazed tone, raising herself on one elbow. "Pregnant! For heaven's sakes, I'm seasick! *Seasick!*" she shouted, then fell back onto the pillow, exhausted by the effort.

"I know that," he said calmly. "I'm only asking because the drug I had in mind shouldn't be given to a woman who is pregnant."

Jami was tired beyond belief, but she found herself unable to keep the sting out of her words. "How did you ever get to be a doctor if you couldn't muddle through the basics of reproduction? In case you didn't know, the end result of what we did last night isn't going to be a *baby!*"

Lance couldn't hold back a smile at her vehemence.

He disappeared into the bathroom and came out a few seconds later with a glass of water.

"Here, take these." He helped her sit up and slipped two small white tablets into her mouth, then held the glass to her lips.

"I really didn't think you were pregnant," he said after she sank down again. "But I had to make sure."

"I know," Jami said with a feeble attempt at a smile. She already regretted leaping to conclusions again, but her mind wasn't exactly in tip-top shape at the moment. "I'm sorry I yelled at you," she added weakly.

Lance shrugged and picked up her hand, turning it palm up in his own. His thumb traced an absent-minded pattern as she closed her eyes, succumbing to the weary demands of her body.

"Don't leave me," she muttered groggily, wishing she could think straight.

She heard a soft chuckle and felt a light touch on her mouth. "I won't," he whispered softly. "I'll stay, as long as you need me." Reassured, she smiled drowsily and slept.

It was early evening when she awoke, and she was alone. She stared at the dimly lit bedroom, not recognizing her surroundings, but at the sound of the surf crashing against the rocky shoreline, the events of the afternoon came back to her.

She breathed a sigh of relief. Her stomach felt abnormally empty, but the queasiness that had plagued her was gone. Despite the hours of sleep, though, her body felt heavy and lethargic. She dragged herself from the bed and staggered toward the bathroom.

A warm shower revived her, but there were still

deep mauve shadows under her wide eyes and the translucence of her skin emphasized the gleaming black of her hair. Lance had put her overnight case in the room while she slept, but she was still too tired to search for a complete change of clothing. She settled for a loosely flowing caftan of jade green velour before running a brush through her hair.

Lance was downstairs in front of a roaring fire, the orange glow of the flames the only source of light in the room. He was lying on a long velvet sofa, his legs stretched out in front of him, both hands clasped around a glass.

He looked so lost in thought that she hated to intrude on him. She paused, one foot still on the spiral staircase, relishing the sight of him and conscious of some strange emotion welling up within her.

A warm feeling radiated from deep inside her as Lance finally noticed her; she walked slowly across the room, unable to take her eyes from his face.

"Feel any better?" He extended a hand to her and drew her down beside him, curling her fingers into his own. His eyes assessed her face carefully.

"Much better," she answered. "Whatever you gave me sure knocked me out, but it really helped my stomach." She shook her head and offered him a tentative smile. "I'm so sorry I got sick. I hope Al Peterson wasn't too upset about cutting short his trial run. He didn't give you a hard time, did he?"

"Not at all." A wry smile tugged his lips upward. "Although I think it may be a while before he takes any more landlubbers aboard."

"He doesn't have to worry about me coming back." Jami laughed shakily. "I'll stick to rowboats from now on, and just for good measure, only ones that are dry-docked."

Lance's smile deepened and his eyes probed hers for a moment. "Are you hungry? I've already eaten, but when I heard the shower I warmed some soup for you."

Jami shook her head. "Thanks, but I'm not sure my stomach is up to food yet."

"Doctor's orders," he said firmly, already rising and striding into the kitchen. "You'll feel worse if your stomach is empty for too long."

She didn't want to argue so she quickly relented, hoping he was right. It turned out he was. After consuming a hearty bowl of thick clam chowder and a sizable chunk of crusty French bread, she felt as if she'd been restored to the ranks of the human race again.

Afterward Lance lay on the floor in front of the huge stone fireplace, arms crossed over his chest as he relaxed against a huge overstuffed pillow. Jami sat on the floor near him, her legs tucked under her, and they idly made small talk.

The quiet and dimly lit surroundings, the popping and hiss of the cedar logs crackling in the grate behind her, the sound of the sea surging against the shore in a motion as old as time itself, all combined to create an atmosphere of peace and serenity unlike any Jami had ever experienced.

It was like a safe harbor, where nothing and no one could harm her, she mused as she listened to Lance's deep, melodious voice. Yet mingled with the tranquility was a curious sense of excitement that tingled along her spine, a strange but not unsettling feeling of expectation.

The feeling intensified further as Jami let her eyes feast on Lance. The dancing light from the flames provided the only illumination in the room, and the firelight cast flickering shadows over the planes and angles of his face, throwing his straight nose and firm hard mouth into prominence.

Her gaze traveled downward. As she caught sight of his hands, now linked together and casually resting on the flat plane of his abdomen, she remembered the feel of his fingers skimming over her body. Equally vivid was her memory of his warm flesh under her own exploring fingertips.

"You aren't even listening to me." Amusement tinged his voice as he asked, "What are you thinking about?"

Far from stopping the wanton flow of her thoughts, the question seemed to incite it further. Tonight was special and she wanted no secrets, no hidden thoughts to come between them.

She tipped her head to one side, her hair spilling sensually forward over one slender shoulder. "I'm not sure you want to know," she said with a teasing half-smile. "It might be a little risqué for your ears."

Lance opened his eyes and his gaze met hers directly before it swept over the length of her body. Her pulse quickened at the flare of masculine appreciation in his eyes. In that instant everything changed. As each acknowledged the potent attraction of the other, the air was suddenly alive with currents fed by the awareness that they were moving toward one very important—and mutual—goal.

A slow smile spread across his face and he placed his hands behind his head with a lazy, indulgent look. "Something tells me you have seduction on the brain. Would you care to comment on the charge, Officer?"

Jami met his lazy look with one of her own, smoothing her hair back with a graceful hand. "That could be rather incriminating," she said softly, not really caring whether they were venturing onto forbidden ground. "I think I'll take the Fifth Amendment."

"Coward," he tossed back. His tone was more of a caress than an accusation and she felt a sudden surge of affection for him. "Since you won't comment on that, tell me something else. Whose seduction were you thinking about—yours or mine?"

A shiver ran through her body at the husky timbre of his voice, but she was enjoying this game of cat and mouse too much to put an end to it so swiftly. She let her eyes travel boldly over his lean-hipped body stretched out on the soft carpet. He looked totally relaxed, but she sensed that at the slightest invitation, the merest provocation, he would spring forth for the chase. And she was only too aware that the victory would belong not only to the hunter, but also to the hunted. At this moment still, she had to admit she wasn't at all sure she wanted the role of the hunted. The thought of seducing Lance, exciting his body as he excited hers, was . . . stimulating, to say the least.

She answered his question with one of her own, shifting forward on her knees to look down at him. Her hands rested lightly on her slim thighs. "Whose seduction would you prefer?"

The long look he gave her sent her pulses careening wildly. She saw burning in his eyes a slow flame that threatened to match the sparks of her own desire, sparks that she no longer attempted to contain. She suddenly yearned for the strength of his body delving into hers, a yearning so intense she felt consumed by its fires. It was a blaze of passion that only Lance could extinguish.

A tremor shook her body as she waited for him to speak, her breath temporarily lodged in her throat.

"I think," he said finally, the merest hint of a smile hovering at the edges of his mouth, "a little of both might satisfy me."

"Might?" she repeated huskily, moistening her lips with the tip of her tongue. "Aren't you sure?"

"There's only one way to find out."

The soft words had no sooner left his mouth than Jami found herself pulled forward in a smooth motion and lying full-length above Lance. His arms were holding her loosely. Their gazes locked together, his demanding, hers questioning, and Jami realized he was waiting for her to take the next step.

"I'm not so sure this is a good idea," she murmured playfully. "It wouldn't surprise me to find that there are any number of women working at the hospital who would be willing to seduce you. Maybe I should let someone else, ah, do the honors."

There was an unrestrained look of hunger in his eyes as he slipped both hands into her silken hair and brought her head down until his mouth was only a breath away from hers. "You're the only one I want touching me," he said softly. "And no other man had better even think about laying a hand on you."

The raw possessiveness in his tone sent a thrill down her spine and she smiled brilliantly at him as she decided to take him up on his invitation to play the aggressor. She pressed tiny tantalizing kisses onto his eyelids, down his cheekbones, and into the hollows under them. Then she fit her body more closely to his. A low growl of satisfaction vibrated in Lance's chest as he brought her mouth to his, still letting her set the pace, and a contented sigh escaped Jami's soft lips at the searing contact. Her small white teeth tugged at his lower lip, then she slowly explored the inner surface of his mouth with a tentative tongue.

A treacherous warmth invaded every cell of her body as Lance's hands roamed slowly up and down her back, and she slipped her hands between their bodies, deftly unfastening the buttons of his shirt. An almost poignant ache began to build inside her, an ache which slowly radiated outward to each and every nerve ending as she slid her fingers through the silky mat of his chest hair, savoring the exquisite feel of muscle and flesh. Aware of Lance's heart beating thunderously against her own, she entwined her legs more closely with his and he eased her onto her side so they were lying face to face.

"Do you know what you do to me?" His lips took hers urgently, the kiss both tender and fierce. "You set me on fire and that's what I want"—again his mouth claimed hers—"to do to you."

"Oh, yes . . . yes, please!" The plea was a low whisper against his neck. Thought was fast becoming impossible as Lance was no longer inclined to submit passively to the touch of her small hands on his body. His passion was as great as her own, communicated to her by the tender yet hungry, gentle but compelling assault of his mouth on hers.

A moan of undeniable need welled up in her as his

hands slid over the soft mounds of her unconfined breasts. His touch was light and maddening, and she ached to feel his hands on her bare skin. Her nipples tingled in response to his elusive caresses, straining upward in search of his touch until at last his hand slid inside her caftan and encompassed one small globe, capturing first one peak and then the other with his exploring fingertips. A sigh of pure satisfaction escaped her lips.

And yet it was not enough. Not nearly enough. Jami succumbed blindly to the flames of passion that rose higher and higher, aware that there could be but one outcome to this night. She needed Lance, needed him to make her complete and whole, as only he could.

Her hand went unerringly to his belt buckle, hurriedly undoing the clasp before reaching for the button of his slacks.

"Jami." His voice was taut with suppressed emotion as his hands squeezed hers. Her movements stilled and he could hear her rapid and shallow breathing, feel the soft rise and fall of her breasts against his chest. Her eyes were drawn upward to his. "Are you sure this is what you want?"

Jami's eyes were nearly molten with need as she gazed trustingly at Lance. His expression was guarded, his tone unexpectedly impassive, and she knew he was trying not to influence this one final, all-important decision for her. Her heart threatened to burst with tenderness as she cradled his lean cheek in her palm. "I've never been more certain of anything in my life," she answered softly. She paused as his words of the night before drifted into her mind. Her tone was little more than a whisper as she added huskily, "I want to share everything with you."

Her words were the catalyst to an explosion and Lance was no longer capable of denying either of them the ultimate pleasure. In seconds they both lay naked before the fire, a plush carpet of burnished copper their bed. Blue eyes aglow with heated passion skimmed over gleaming silken curves, a pale gold silhouette in the shadow of the dancing flames. Unrestrained desire flickered through Jami as she felt the sinewy length of his taut male body against the yielding softness of her own, and she gloried in the compelling swell of masculine arousal that was urgently pressing into her curves.

Lance traced the slender lines of her body from breast to thigh, his hand resting possessively on the swell of her hip as he breathed, "You're exquisite . . ." He reached up to smooth the strands of hair falling across her breast, lingered on the gentle curve which filled his palm. ". . . shiny black silk on smooth ivory satin . . . beautiful!"

Her long lashes lifted slowly and she gazed in wonder at the lean hard form that she knew would soon bring her to rapturous fulfillment. The firelight lent an orange glow to the rippling male magnificence of his body, to the smooth corded muscles encased in gleaming bronze flesh. He seemed almost godlike to Jami.

And she loved him. She knew it instinctively and made no effort to hide what she was feeling as she drank her fill of his body. Only love could trigger this wild singing in her heart, this all-consuming desire to be bound to Lance, to have their spirits linked together in a total union of body and soul.

He made love to her slowly, patiently, as if they had all the time in the world. Hands as gentle as a feather stroked the fullness of her breasts, brushed over the flat planes of her stomach before descending to tantalize the sweetness of her femininity with a slow, tortuous, but exquisite motion that sent her drowning in waves of pleasure.

Finally she could stand no more. She opened her eyes and gazed at him beseechingly. In that moment, hearing his breath as ragged and tormented as her own, she knew his passion and hers matched in ferocity.

Her small hands clutched his shoulders and she arched her body blindly toward him. "Love me, Lance," she cried weakly, breathlessly, "love me."

His hoarse response was lost as his arms tightened around her body, lifted her gently, tenderly, claimed her completely as his own.

What had gone before was but a spine-tingling shiver as a wild feeling of elation captured her, swept her up in a tempest of desire, carried her ever higher into a raging vortex of fire and flame. Her body was ablaze with passion as she was hurled even deeper into a world of spinning sensations and exquisite delight.

There was neither tormentor nor tormented, vanquisher nor vanquished, conqueror nor conquered. The deep physical satisfaction achieved by each was only a part of their union. The giving, the taking, the sharing they experienced all blended together to form a bond, a harmony of both body and mind which transcended description.

Long after the storm burst in a pulsating tide of delight, Jami lay curled within the circle of Lance's arms, her head pillowed on his shoulder. The fire cast its coppery glow over the room and she felt sated and peaceful, though perhaps a little overwhelmed, as she basked contentedly in his arms, savoring a sense of unity and oneness with Lance. The feeling was unique and priceless. She knew now, beyond any doubt, how very much she loved him.

"I didn't intend for this to happen, you know." Lance's voice was low, with a hint of uncharacteristic uncertainty. He absently stroked her hair and cradled her slender body even closer.

"I know," she said quietly, a frown creasing her brow for an instant. Was he apologizing—or making excuses?

"I'm not sorry it did, though," he said evenly, tipping her face up to his. He hesitated for a fraction of a second. "Are you?"

Jami was acutely aware of the sudden rigidity in the arms that held her. She searched his eyes, taken aback by the low vibrant quality of his voice, and realized that a negative response from her could trigger feelings of guilt in him, feelings he had no reason to experience.

She touched her lips to his, a dreamy smile of contentment curving her mouth. "No, I'm not sorry," she whispered, one hand trailing down the slightly roughened line of his jaw. "It was beautiful . . . something I'll never forget," she added shyly. As if she ever could, loving him the way she did.

"I'm not about to let you," he muttered into her hair. His hold tightened fiercely for a second before his eyes impaled her own. "This changes everything between us. I hope you're aware of that."

"I—I know," she admitted rather unsteadily, a little confused by the turbulent swirl of emotions his words aroused. She couldn't pretend that tonight had never happened, and didn't *want* to. But she knew the future held no promises, much as she wished it could be different.

She met his gaze hesitantly. "Let's just take it a day at a time, okay? No pressure tactics on either side."

Lance watched her closely and she knew he was aware of her uncertainty and doubt. "All right," he finally acquiesced with a shake of his head. "I'll settle for that." His eyes lingered on her lips, which parted in a grateful smile, before dropping to creamy bare shoulders exposed above the blanket he had pulled over them. "In the meantime," he added softly, "we have the rest of the night to get through. Any ideas on where to spend it?"

Jami's heart took a dangerous leap at the warm intimacy of his look. Something pagan deep inside her responded and she ran her fingers across his taut abdomen, her nails lightly raking through the springy dark hair before venturing lower, delighting in his firm body as she continued her bold exploration.

"I think"—her voice was breathless as she answered him—"bed would be the logical place."

Lance covered her hand with his own, stilling the motion of her fingers just short of their goal. "Considering the fact that you slept the afternoon away, I hope that wasn't what you had in mind, at least for the next—"

"Day or so?" She smiled provocatively at him and

slipped her leg seductively over his, twining her arms around his neck as she moved her body above his.

"No," she said softly, lowering her mouth to brush across his, gazing at him with eyes that glowed with longing, "it wasn't . . ."

Chapter Nine

It was hard to come back to earth after such an idyllic weekend, Jami mused on Monday morning as she buttoned her uniform shirt in the tiny ex-interview room that now served as the women's locker room. No more peaceful walks on a secluded beach, with the roar of the surf echoing in the background; no more quiet cozy dinners in front of a blazing fire; no more nights nestled securely within Lance's arms . . . at least not until Wednesday. Lance was leaving later that afternoon for a conference in Seattle.

With that thought lingering in her mind, she closed her locker with a controlled slam, a smile of anticipation curving her lips as she headed for the morning briefing.

In the conference room where the shift was rapidly

gathering, she prepared for the day's activities, selecting a hand-held radio and car keys, stamping her notebook with the date. She paid little attention to the buzzing din of male voices around her. By now she was used to the idle banter, which was often slightly off-color, and she accepted the fact that it came with the territory.

But when she crossed the room to take a seat at the long Formica-topped table, something of her buoyant and self-satisfied mood must have conveyed itself to her male counterparts. She found herself on the receiving end of more than a few curious stares.

"Hey, what gives?" she asked with a laugh. "I'm not the new kid on the block, you know. I've been a member of the family for three years now, remember?"

"Yeah, but you never looked like you do today." Dan Marino, who'd graduated with her from the Police Academy, turned his sharp gaze on her. "You look like you've just had a month's vacation on a warm sunny island in the Caribbean. Minus the tan, of course," he added with a grin.

"You'd be surprised what a few days at one of Oregon's own beaches will do," she murmured with a secretive smile. "Much closer and a lot cheaper than a trip to the Caribbean."

"Hah!" snorted a voice from the back of the room. "A good woman to wake up with in the morning will accomplish the same damn thing. Or maybe I should say a good man, eh, Simpson?"

She recognized the voice as Brian Thompson's. There was a man whose manner left much to be desired. She and Thompson had had more than a few go-rounds on the subject of brute force versus subtle logic and reasoning. His motto seemed to be "act now, think later," and they often disagreed on the usefulness of such a plan given a particular situation.

Today, however, even Thompson's sly innuendos couldn't shatter her good humor. "I'll never tell," she said, lifting her slender shoulders and sending him a sweet smile. She almost laughed aloud as his jaw dropped. Clearly he'd expected her usual fiery retort to his barb, and she absently considered changing her tactics where he was concerned. Maybe a woman's gentle cajolery could bring him around to her way of thinking.

There was little time that day to think of Lance or the past weekend. Her mind was occupied with the investigation of several burglaries which occurred as soon as she had hit the street. One call followed another, and it was mid-afternoon before she took a breather, albeit a very short one. She had just stopped the squad car in front of a fast-food restaurant for her first break of the day and was reaching for the microphone to obtain clearance when the call came through.

"452, 399 . . . 12-42 at 3204 Southview. Verbal only at this time . . . Code two."

"Just what I need—a family fight with Brian Thompson as a partner," she muttered as she picked up the mike. "452, 12-4," she said crisply.

A frown puckered her brow as she swung the squad car into the flow of traffic. She recognized the address as one she'd been to on several occasions just prior to Christmas on the same type of call. Both times the argument had died down for the most part by the time the police had arrived, but on the last occasion Jami had spotted a cut on Lillian Wyler's temple.

While another officer calmed her husband, Jami had drawn the woman aside and queried her about the cut, but Mrs. Wyler had vehemently denied that her husband had had anything to do with it. Jami couldn't prove anything without the woman's testimony, but she had tactfully let Mrs. Wyler know that she didn't have to put up with any physical abuse, making sure she understood that she could seek advice, as well as temporary shelter, at the Women's Crisis Center.

Thompson was parked a few houses away from the Wyler residence when Jami pulled her cruiser into the street five minutes later.

"I thought we had a live one, but it seems to have fizzled out," he said when she joined him on the sidewalk. "A neighbor came out a minute ago and told me they've been going strong for the last half hour, but I haven't heard any commotion since I got here."

"The neighbor phoned in the call?" Jami asked as they hurried toward a two-story house that was sadly in need of a paint job.

"Yeah," confirmed Thompson. "She said the husband lost his job a few months ago and he and the wife have been going at it ever since."

Jami nodded. "I responded to a couple of calls here before Christmas, but there wasn't much of a ruckus going on when we arrived. The husband got a little overzealous a few days before the last call, but she wouldn't say a word against him."

"They never do," Thompson said. "Or else they bail the guy out as soon as he's booked in on the charges."

Jami couldn't help agreeing with Thompson in this instance. His words were only too true. Why any woman would put up with such treatment, she couldn't figure out, but she'd seen it happen on more occasions than she cared to remember.

"Do me a favor, Thompson," she said as they mounted the rickety wooden steps onto the porch. "Let me do the talking if things get rough, okay? The husband was pretty mouthy the last time I was here and we don't need a fistfight on our hands."

"What?" Thompson mocked softly from behind her. "No confidence in my powers of persuasion? Believe me, Simpson, I can be very eloquent when the occasion warrants it."

When? Jami wondered as she raised a hand to knock on the door. When you're trying to lure some poor unsuspecting woman into your bed?

But there was little time to think about Thompson's self-professed oratorical abilities because the front door of the house was thrown open. Jami's sharp eyes took in Lillian Wyler's distraught features. Her thin hand was dabbing at a stream of blood flowing from a cut in her upper lip with a clean but nearly threadbare handkerchief. Over Mrs. Wyler's shoulder Jami could see two small boys huddled in the corner, their eyes wide with fear. Poor kids, Jami thought, having to see their parents at each other's throats like this.

She smiled reassuringly at them, then turned back to their mother. "May we come in, Mrs. Wyler? I understand you and your husband are having a problem this afternoon. My partner and I would like to talk to you for a few minutes to make sure everything's okay."

The woman motioned Jami and Thompson inside. They were standing in a small living room. The furnishings were rather shabby, but under the drab oval braided rug, the wooden floor was clean and shining from tedious hours of hand waxing. Jami certainly couldn't fault Mrs. Wyler for the home she maintained for her husband and children. She was obviously making the best of a bad situation. Jami wondered if the spat had erupted for the same reason it had started before—Bill Wyler's drinking and failure to look for a job.

"I should have listened to you, Officer Simpson," the tiny woman muttered. "I never should have stayed here and let that damn husband of mine walk all over me. I don't know why I didn't clear out then! All I've had is weeks and weeks of working my fingers to the bone during the day and waiting tables at night, while that bastard goes down to the bar on the corner and drinks away all my hard-earned money."

"You're working now, Mrs. Wyler?" queried Jami, a little surprised at the quiet woman's outburst.

"Yes." The woman dabbed at the cut, but held her head high. "The pay isn't much, but it's better than living off the state.

"He hasn't even been looking for a job, not since the first week he was laid off at the lumber mill. And at least four times a week he goes out boozing and then comes back drunk and meaner than hell! I can't take it anymore." The woman shook her head despairingly. "I just can't take it."

Jami raised her brows and glanced at Thompson, who was wearing a surprisingly sympathetic expression. He cleared his throat and looked around the room. "Where is your husband, by the way?"

"Don't know and don't care," Mrs. Wyler said sullenly. "After he hit me, he ran out the back door. I hope he never comes back! It'll save me the trouble of leaving!"

"What the hell are you cops doing on my property?"

Three heads swiveled in the direction of the gravelly voice. Though the words were slightly slurred, the vicious tone was unmistakable. Bill Wyler stood in the kitchen doorway, his shirttail hanging outside his crumpled jeans, his feet bare. A growth of beard darkened his thin cheeks. Even from her position ten feet away from him, Jami could smell the stench of alcohol.

"You're the one who's not welcome here, you bastard!" Mrs. Wyler screeched at him. "The police came because *I* wanted them here!"

"They got no right to interfere in our business," the man growled. "Now get rid of them!"

"Not until I'm good and ready," Lillian Wyler announced defiantly. If the situation hadn't been quite so grim, Jami might have applauded her spunk. As it was, she had a feeling Mrs. Wyler was acting brave in front of her husband because of the presence of two uniformed officers at her side. "In fact, I think they can just take you along with them when they leave." She turned to Jami and indicated the gash on her lip. "There's a law against what he did to me, isn't there?"

"Yes, there is," Jami answered slowly, "but—"

"Then arrest him! Arrest him and take him to jail! He can rot there forever for all I care!"

Jami sighed. It was true there were sufficient grounds for an arrest; in fact, the law required it in Oregon in cases like this. But Wyler was hardly likely to learn a lesson from it if Lillian was going to beat her to the booking desk with his bail money. And she had to admit Mrs. Wyler was apt to do just that, considering her past record.

Jami glanced at Thompson, her expression conveying to him the unspoken message to draw Mrs. Wyler aside and ascertain her intentions before they took Bill Wyler into custody. He nodded and gently nudged the woman toward the hallway.

A movement in Jami's peripheral vision caught her attention even as her senses, attuned to the possibility of impending disaster, screamed a warning. She pivoted, her fingers reaching instinctively toward her holster, and though she was quick, Bill Wyler was quicker. That all-important fraction of a second had given him the edge.

Her fingers fell away from the holster as she acknowledged to herself that that course of action was no longer available to her. She pushed aside the sickening feeling of fear that threatened to swamp her good judgment. If she was going to get out of this alive, she needed all her faculties intact. She'd had a lot of varied experiences during her years with the Department, but this one was a first.

Her gaze rose from the small caliber gun Bill Wyler had pulled from his belt and which was now leveled directly at her chest. She was totally unaware of Lillian Wyler's shocked gasp and of the two children who sat terror-stricken on the couch. As for Thompson, she could only pray he wouldn't do anything rash.

Thankfully, he didn't reach for either his radio or his gun, undoubtedly because both of them, and Mrs. Wyler, too, were an easy target for Wyler. Drunk or not, they couldn't take any chances with his aim. She knew intuitively that Thompson's sharp eyes were trained on Wyler, that he was poised and ready to spring into action the second she needed him. She could only hope it wouldn't come to that.

Praying that Wyler wasn't intoxicated to the point of being totally unreachable, she said, "Now wait a minute, Bill." To her relief, her voice was quiet but even. "I want you to think about things for a minute here before you do anything you'll regret later."

"You're gonna haul me off to jail! That's reason enough in my book to put a stop to it. I ain't a criminal and I don't wanna be treated like one!"

A cold sweat broke out on Jami's brow as she recognized the dogged determination in his tone. Somehow she had to get out of this without anyone being hurt or killed—but how?

"Look," she said slowly, her mind racing as she chose her words carefully. She could afford no mistakes. One chance was all she had! "I'm not going to lie to you. You're right about my partner and I taking you to jail, but all you'll be facing is an assault charge. Since it's your first offense, you'll probably end up on probation. But if you kill me, you'll be up against a first-degree murder charge. And instead of spending a night in jail, you'll spend a lifetime in prison." There was a tense pause as she let him absorb her words. "Is that what you want, Bill? To have your children think of you as a man who killed another human being? To see them through a glass window a few times a month, never being able to hold them, to touch them . . . never being around when they need you? Is that what you want for yourself? And for them?"

Wyler's bloodshot eyes stared at her for a long, tension-filled moment. Finally he spoke. "No." His voice was hoarse, little more than a croak. "I love my boys." His eyes flickered toward his wife, then came back to Jami. "I love Lilly too. Only . . . these last few months I—I guess I ain't been taking care of my family like I should have." One shaky hand reached up and rubbed the stubble on his chin. "I guess I been drinking too much. Lilly and I always got along fine until the mill closed and I lost my job."

"You probably felt like a failure," Jami said gently. "I'm sure it happens to the best of us at one time or another. Granted, it affects each person differently, but in your case I think you should know that there are people who care and are willing to help, if you'll let them."

To her immense relief, she noticed the barrel of the gun wavering as Wyler's grip on it loosened. Now—*now* was the time to take advantage of the remorse she was sure was tearing at his insides.

"An employment counselor might be able to help you find work," she continued. "They know the job market better than anyone. And I understand that if a person qualifies, there are on-the-job training programs that pay a reduced wage while you're learning a skill. And as for the drinking problem, there are organizations that can help you with that too."

She took a deep, quivering breath, gathered all her courage, and took one step forward, then another. This was the moment of decision and she could only hope that a force higher than any on earth was watching over her.

"Give me the gun, Bill," she said gently, still moving forward slowly. "Otherwise, no one can help you."

The gun was dangling loosely in his grasp when she finally reached him, and she took it from him gently. His red-rimmed eyes held an expression of regret, as well as guilt, but also a faint hint of hope— hope that hadn't been there before. Feeling curiously weak-kneed, Jami emptied six hollow-point bullets from the pistol's chamber into her palm before placing the gun in her gunbelt. Then she retreated a step and watched as Mrs. Wyler and Thompson simultaneously rushed toward Wyler, somehow not surprised to see that the light of battle in Lillian Wyler's eyes had been replaced by a bright shimmer of tears as she embraced her husband.

Thompson looked over Wyler's shoulder at Jami as he snapped a pair of handcuffs in place. "Nice job, Simpson."

Jami managed a wobbly smile in response to the brief look of admiration in his eyes. She just might make a believer out of him yet, she thought to herself as she pulled a Miranda card from her pocket and read Wyler his rights, but she certainly hoped it wouldn't take another incident like this to accomplish it. Once in a lifetime was enough . . .

By the time Jami entered her apartment early that evening, the incident had taken its toll. She felt exhausted, both mentally and physically, yet taut as a bowstring.

After grabbing a quick bite to eat in the kitchen, she dragged herself into the living room and switched on the television. She settled into her favorite leather chair, carelessly draped one slim leg over the arm, and listened with half an ear to the droning voice of the newscaster, drawing in a series of long deep breaths in an effort to relax. It seemed she had just succeeded in freeing her mind of all conscious thought, quite a feat in light of her hectic day, when a trio of melodic notes from her doorbell resounded in the room.

With an exasperated sigh she lifted herself from the chair and headed toward the front door, not really relishing the thought of visitors. But when she threw open the door, surprise and pleasure lit up her tired eyes.

"Lance!" She quickly moved aside so he could come in. Closing the door, she leaned against it and let her gaze skim over his tall body appreciatively, noting the way his broad shoulders filled his fawn-colored suede jacket and how his dark brown slacks molded his lean hips and thighs. The memory of his smooth hair-roughened skin that she knew lay under the cloth caused her breath to catch in her throat, and she wondered if her reaction to him would always be this profound.

Yet as her eyes lifted to meet his and noted the grim expression on his face, a tingle of apprehension snaked down her spine.

She shifted a little uncomfortably, but her gaze never left his. "I thought you were leaving for Seattle this evening."

Lance's jaw tightened and his mouth thinned. "I was," he said tersely. "But when I heard about your little escapade, I booked a later flight."

"Escapade?" she echoed, her brows drawing together.

"I'm talking about this afternoon when you nearly got yourself killed!" he cut in sharply. Jami's eyes widened at his abrupt tone, and Lance grabbed her narrow shoulders and gave her a brief shake.

She was too surprised to be angry. "I take it you're

talking about the man who pulled a gun on me," she said, somehow feeling guilty, though she knew she had no reason to be.

"You're damn right I am," he said, his voice rough with anxiety. His eyes smoldered down at her, his expression darkening even more, as if he were in acute pain. His fingers curled tightly into the soft flesh of her upper arms. "My God," he muttered, closing his eyes. His voice was low and choked, almost subdued, in sharp contrast to his earlier gruffness. "When I think of what could have happened . . ." He opened his eyes and looked down at her. Jami was struck to the core by the depth of emotion reflected in the crystal blue of his eyes.

Her heart fluttered, then began to soar as she comprehended his startling reaction to the incident. He was concerned, very concerned. That was only too obvious. Could it be that he cared for her, more than she had thought? She hardly dared to hope, even to breathe.

But first she had to set his mind at ease. With a calm assurance that belied her inner turmoil, she led him over to the sofa and sat down beside him.

"Lance," she said, laying a hand lightly on his shoulder. She felt his muscles tighten under the suede covering and his reaction sent a stab of dismay through her, but she kept her hand where it was. "I think you're blowing this way out of proportion." She paused briefly. "How did you hear about it anyway?"

He made an impatient gesture with his hand. "The local news report on my way to the airport in Portland."

Jami shrugged. "Well, you know the news media, always making a mountain out of a molehill. Somehow they manage to make things sound worse than they actually are."

"Don't give me that! You're the one who's trying to downplay this whole thing and you know it. You've already admitted the guy had a gun pointed at you!"

Her gaze dropped quickly and her hand fell to her lap. She twisted her fingers together guiltily. "Well . . ."

"And the gun was loaded, with bullets in the chamber, right?"

Jami winced a little at his cutting tone and bit her lip, nodding slowly in affirmation. He was making her feel like the accused when all she was trying to do was reassure him.

"And he could have pulled the trigger *at any time*, couldn't he?"

She lifted pleading eyes to his taut features. "Yes, but—"

"I rest my case," he interrupted her coldly. "He could have killed you. Now tell me that's an exaggeration."

Jami returned his glare with a level look of her own. He was right and there was no use trying to convince him he wasn't. "I can't and you know it," she said evenly. "The point is I wasn't hurt, and that's what matters."

With a savage oath Lance got up from the sofa and started pacing around the room like a caged animal. Finally he stopped in front of her, jamming his hands deep into his pockets. "How can you be so calm about it?" he asked in a harsh, raw voice, clearly exasperated. "How can you just sit there, as if . . . as if the whole thing had never happened! My God, woman, are you made of steel? Next you'll be telling me what a hrill you got out of being in such a dangerous ituation."

"No, it wasn't a thrill." She leaned her head against he back of the sofa, suddenly feeling very tired again. A person who says he feels no fear is either a fool or a iar, and I'm neither." She hesitated for a second, ;roping for the right words. "I was afraid, more afraid han I've ever been in my whole life. But if I had let my ear dominate me, it's possible I might not have come)ut alive. For my own self-preservation, I had to let hat man know I was in control, that I wasn't going to illow him to manipulate me. And if I wasn't aware of ny own fear and wasn't able to overcome it, I'd be a lamn poor police officer. I simply can't allow myself to lwell on it or I'd never be able to spend another day on :he job."

Lance stared at her for a long moment in tense silence, his expression hidden in the shadowed glow of the lamplight behind him. Then he sat down heav-ily beside her, wrapping an arm around her and pulling her close.

To Jami, it was a homecoming, a much-needed shelter from the hair-raising events of the day, events that had shaken her far more than she was willing to admit, even to herself. She rubbed her cheek against his jacket, nestling her face into his neck and breath-ing in his clean male scent mingled with the spicy aroma of his cologne.

A contented smile tipped her lips upward, but the smile faded when Jami opened her eyes and saw Lance's grimly set features and an oddly pained look in his eyes.

"You're still angry, aren't you?" she asked softly. "Please don't be. I was only doing my job and I . . . I don't take unnecessary risks. Surely you know me well enough to realize that."

Lance ran a hand through his hair. "I'm not angry, just upset." He got up and began pacing again while Jami watched, growing more puzzled by the moment at his uncharacteristic behavior.

Again he stopped in front of her. "It's not *your* actions I'm worried about so much as the other guy's," he said grimly. "There are a lot of unpredictable, selfish, crazy people in this world who don't give a damn about anyone else. And you have to admit, people like that have no qualms whatsoever about robbing a person of what he treasures most—"

"His life," Jami interjected softly, fully aware of what Lance was getting at. "And especially a cop's life, right?"

He nodded, his lips set in a straight, uncompromising line. His gaze met hers head on, challenging her to refute her own statement.

She held up a conciliatory hand. "Believe me, I'm fully aware of it," she said dryly, then added, "Maybe I should have been a fire fighter. You know, friend of the people rather than foe."

Her attempt to relieve the strained atmosphere failed miserably, leaving her a little uncertain as to what to say next. She stared up at Lance and sighed.

"Lance, I appreciate your concern, but as you can see, I'm perfectly fine!"

"This time! You might not be so lucky the next."

Jami sat up abruptly, her small chin jutting out sharply. "Don't you think maybe you're carrying this a little far?"

"No!" he shot back. "I don't think you realize what a dangerous profession you're in!"

"How can you say that when all this time you've been accusing me of being suspicious—and laying the blame on my job!" She jumped up and faced him squarely. "What you don't seem to realize is that situations like the one today don't crop up on a daily basis, even though we have to be prepared for them. This isn't New York City or Chicago."

"It's not the Garden of Eden either!"

The tension in the air was almost crackling in its intensity as icy blue eyes collided with blazing gold ones for endless moments. Then suddenly all the fight went out of Jami, leaving her feeling weak inside. Lance was standing with his hands braced on his hips, staring at her in expectant silence, a muscle twitching in his cheek.

He looked hard and unyielding, totally unapproachable, and suddenly Jami wanted desperately to recapture what they had shared these last days. She wanted them to be friends, lovers . . .

She took a faltering step toward him, uncertainty mingling with the silent plea in her eyes. "Lance, I . . . please . . ."

The next instant she found herself wrapped in his embrace, her cheek crushed against his chest. A shudder went through his body and she knew a brief spiraling joy, aware that the events of the day had had no less an impact on him than on her.

"Lance," she whispered recklessly, "what time does your plane leave?"

"Ten-thirty," he answered above her head.

Already her restless fingers had slipped his jacket off his broad shoulders and dropped it on the chair at his side. She didn't really care if he thought her wanton or bold. Her need to be reassured of his desire for her, the need to love and be loved, was too great.

But his hand closed over hers as she began u do-ing the buttons of his shirt, halting her movements. She looked up at him questioningly, a slight frown forming as she sensed two warring factions deep within him. One was manifested by the blaze of passion which flared in his eyes, the other by the uncompromising set of the mouth that she wished would possess her own until nothing else mattered but blinding, searing desire. Somehow, she had to help influence his decision, and she knew only one way.

Pride was all but forgotten as she stood on tiptoe and slipped her arms around his neck, tangling her fingers in the thick blond hair at his neck and tug-ging his head down to hers. Her mouth opened on his, seeking, searching to rediscover the secrets only his hands, his lips, his body could lay bare.

For long, timeless seconds their bodies were in har-mony as each relived precious moments of ecstasy they had shared only the day before. Jami's soft curves eagerly melded into the lean angular contours of Lance's body, quiveringly and achingly aware of the hard male thrust pressing into the softness of her stomach. A tremor wracked her slender body. Lord, how she wanted him . . . here . . . now . . .

Suddenly her arms were thrust down to her sides and ruthlessly held in place when she would have wound them again around his body.

"This isn't right," he said thickly, shaking his head. "I shouldn't even be here. I should be on my way to the airport."

Confused by his words, dazed by his rejection, the

words came tumbling out in a breathless whisper before she could stop them. "Why? Why don't you want to make love to me?"

The break in her voice at the last was unmistakable, and Lance closed his eyes briefly, one hand releasing her wrist to smooth the tumbled waves of her hair. His breathing was harsh, his tone raspy, as he muttered, "If you only knew how much I want to. . . . But I can't."

"Why not?" The question ripped from Jami's lips as her eyes searched his face, seeking an answer. Why was tonight different from the blissful weekend at the beach? But instead of an answer, she saw only guilt and pain reflected on his chiseled features. Then, and only then, did the flames of passion kindled by the first brush of her fingertips across his skin begin to wane, fading first to embers, then to a cold gray ash which left a gnawing, empty feeling deep inside her.

"Don't you see, Jami, I just can't! Not when I'm not even sure there's a tomorrow for us—" He broke off and took a deep breath, realizing how badly he was handling this. Jami looked so lost and alone, his heart felt as if it were being torn in two. He reached for her, but let his hands fall limply to his sides as she shrank from him.

Jami heard his words through a haze of pain, but some inner strength she hadn't known she possessed rose to the surface. She lifted her head to meet his agonized stare. "You're not sure there's a tomorrow for us," she repeated slowly. "What you're saying is that . . . this is the end." Her words were clear, her tone even and calm, but she felt as if she were floating outside of herself, that it was another Jami Simpson who, to all appearances, couldn't care less that the man she loved was . . . But no, *no!* She couldn't say it, couldn't even think it . . .

Lance dropped into a chair, his shoulders slumping wearily. He rested his forehead on his hand for a moment. When he finally spoke, his voice was a strange blend of resignation laced with regret.

"I'm sorry, Jami"—he hesitated for a breathless, heart-stopping second before delivering his blow—"but maybe now is as good a time as any for us to call it quits."

Jami froze, her eyes wide and disbelieving, her skin clammy and cold as death. The tip of her tongue moistened her dry lips before she was able to speak. "I don't understand," she said woodenly, afraid to look at him, afraid *not* to look at him. This could very well be the last time she would ever see him. What had she done?

Unknowingly she had voiced the question aloud. Unable to help himself, Lance pulled her stiff body down beside him, turning her face into his chest. He clasped ice-cold fingers in a fierce grip, making no effort to mask the torment he was feeling.

"You haven't done anything," he said heavily. "It's something I should have seen coming long ago, but I didn't. Or maybe it was just that I didn't want to."

Her halting whisper stopped him for a second. "I . . . you're not making any sense. I—"

"Jami, there's no easy way to say this and I wish I didn't have to." He tipped her face upward. "Until this afternoon I intended to ask you to marry me."

Marriage! The announcement should have sent elation spinning through her. Instead the sadness lurking in his eyes caused a cold knot of fear to form in her stomach. She opened her mouth to speak, but a finger against her lips prevented any sound from forming.

"When we first met," he said quietly, "you were determined to tread lightly. Now"—he hesitated—"I'm the one who's running scared." He held up a hand as she started to speak. "No, let me finish.

"I don't ever again want to experience a day like today." His voice shook with the force of his emotions, emotions that were not lost on Jami, trembling at his side. "All I could think was what if you had died?" The seconds ticked by in tense silence before he was able to continue. A tender hand grazed Jami's cheek. "Don't you see?" he asked gently. "I just don't think I could take it if that happened again. That's why maybe we should call it off now, before we're beyond the point of no return."

But I'm beyond that point already, she wanted to cry, to plead with him. *I love you! Doesn't that count for anything?*

"My job," she said, her tone far from steady, "you're talking about my job."

Lance nodded in despair. "Every time you walked out the door, I'd wonder if it would be the last time I'd ever see you. I'd wonder—"

"Other people learn to cope, Lance. Any police wife can tell you—"

"How dangerous a job it is," he cut in. "*Coping* is not accepting, and I'm afraid I'd never be able to accept the fact that you put your life on the line every day you report to work."

"But, Lance—"

"There are no buts about it," he interrupted savagely. "How many bullets do you have to dodge before you realize the world isn't filled with fun-loving banner-toting boy scouts?" He groaned and buried his head in his hands. "What am I saying! It's what you've been trying to tell me all along."

Jami took a deep tremulous breath, trying to control her emotions. He just couldn't understand that she knew how to take care of herself! But wait—she didn't have to argue with him!

Impulsively she leaned forward, a soft glow in her eyes as she laid a placating hand on his arm. "It doesn't have to be like this, Lance. I could quit, or at least transfer to another job in the Department that would keep me off the streets . . ."

Her words trailed off as he shook his head, and again she witnessed that strange sadness lingering in the back of his eyes. She recognized the grim look of determination even before he spoke.

"No."

"But why? I'd do anything for you—for us."

"No, I won't let you do that!" He practically threw himself from the sofa, his tormented gaze holding her motionless. "I don't want you to have to make a choice like that. You'd hate me for it eventually!"

She shook her head. "No, I could never—"

"I know how much your job means to you and I won't let you do it. What kind of a future would we have?" he demanded. "I don't want you to have to give up your work for me. You'd end up resenting me, and with that hanging between us, there's no way we could maintain a solid relationship. It would be like—like trying to build a city of skyscrapers on acres of quicksand!"

Jami could only stare up at him mutely, her mouth trembling. She blinked hard to hold back the tears.

All her dreams, dreams of a future with Lance, were being shattered and torn to shreds.

She watched as he grabbed his coat, his face an iron mask of grim determination. There would be no changing his mind—she knew him well enough to know it was useless to try. He was too firm, too staunch in his beliefs. And he was only too sure of the emotions that had driven him to this painful parting.

Running scared. The phrase would have been laughable if she hadn't been shriveling up inside with each step that took him closer to the door. The irony of the situation was that it was Lance's persistence, his patience, that had drawn her out of the niche she had unknowingly placed herself in. He had enticed her, persuaded her, showed her that love was worth any and all risks.

But now it was all falling apart in front of her. She couldn't let him go without one last attempt. . . .

"Lance," she cried as he flung open the door and was about to step into the night. "Wh-when will I see you again?"

She could see his back stiffen as he halted, one hand still on the doorknob. He made no move to turn back to her.

"I don't know, Jami. I just don't know."

He sounded so tired, so defeated, that at that moment Jami knew the battle was over and the war was lost. The injustice of it suddenly turned to anger and she took a step forward, her hands clenched tightly at her sides.

"You don't care about me at all," she accused his broad back, her voice unnaturally hoarse. "You never did . . . you lied . . . dammit, you lied!"

Lance finally turned his head to look at her. His

voice was as hollow as she felt inside. "Oh, I care. I care . . . too much."

And then he was gone. She was left alone—alone with a deafening silence that grew steadily until she felt as if she were suffocating. A chill that had nothing to do with the cool rush of air gushing into the room with the opening and closing of the door pervaded her limbs and she began to tremble.

Absolute trust . . . blind faith . . . What had she done? She had believed in him, trusted him, put all her faith in him. And for what? For this?

Chapter Ten

The last day in February was beautiful. The air was crisp and clear, and the temperature in the mid-sixties, unseasonably warm for late winter. The sunshine seemed to have cast its spell over everyone. Throughout the city Jami could hear carefree laughter as she cruised back to the station to work on a report. The entire population of the city seemed to be happy—with one exception.

The month had been a difficult one for Jami—both at work and at home. It was painful, this thing called love. But she was strong and she was determined to put it behind her and start over. But would she ever trust again?

Her expression was grim as she parked her squad

car in the underground garage and walked briskly toward the stairway.

"Jami! Wait up!"

She turned at the sound of the masculine voice, and for the first time in weeks a genuine smile warmed her features as she recognized Ron Sloan's tall, lanky figure striding toward her. Ron had been her trainer during her probationary period with the Department.

"Hi, Coach," she greeted him as he came up to her, a grin creasing his thin face. She eyed his three-piece business suit and neatly trimmed chestnut hair, and gave him a speculative look. "You look dressed to kill. No drug busts today?"

"Nope," he said cheerfully. "My masquerading days are finally over, thank heavens. I'm off the drug team and back to an eight-to-five stint in Detectives."

"And not a moment too soon, from the sound of it," Jami surmised. "I take it Linda didn't appreciate the irregular hours you kept."

"Among other things," Ron said with a lift of his brows. "She was getting a little tired of having dinners interrupted and being roused by 2:00 A.M. phone calls. For a while it was almost as bad as having a newborn baby in the house again. Anyway"—he rubbed his chin and laughed—"I'm one of those strange guys who doesn't mind shaving twice a day, so going around with a two-day growth of beard was beginning to get to me, to say nothing of Linda's complaints about having a Brillo pad for a husband."

Jami couldn't hold back a laugh. "Now that's a problem we female officers don't have to contend with," she pointed out. "Maybe the Vice Squad should be made up of women instead of men."

Ron's expression grew serious as he gazed down at her in the dim light. "Don't tell me you're actually thinking about—"

"No way," she assured him. "Even if there were an opening on the drug team, I wouldn't consider applying for it. Patrol suits me just fine." For now, she added to herself silently. Ever since the breach between her and Lance, her police work no longer provided the personal satisfaction, the excitement it had offered before. She knew it was because her job was primarily responsible for the rift, and she could only hope her feelings would pass and she could immerse herself in her work with her usual fervor once more. It was all she had now.

She swallowed the strange lump in her throat and managed a smile for Ron, who was watching her closely.

He cleared his throat and nodded. "It's not that I don't think you couldn't handle it—I know you could. But Vice isn't for everyone." He paused as if weighing his words carefully. "You're a good cop, Jami. But then, I'm sure you know that."

Jami couldn't help being pleased at his praise. She'd always felt that she and Ron operated on the same level. He had never accorded her any preferential treatment because of her sex, nor had he attempted to foist upon her the viewpoint that a man, any man, was better suited for the job.

She smiled at him. "You deserve some of the credit for that."

"Only some?" He lifted an eyebrow, rubbing his chin thoughtfully. "You know," he began, "there was a time I thought you wouldn't make it."

Jami saw the gleam of laughter in his eyes, but she played along. "Oh? And just when was that?"

"Remember the time on the graveyard shift when I forgot my lunch at home and we went back to my house to get it?"

"The first time I ever drove the patrol car," she recalled. "I stayed in the car while you went inside for your lunch—"

"And dropped it all on the sidewalk when I ran back outside because you had turned on the overheads and siren for heaven only knows what reason!"

"I was curious about the switches and you hadn't bothered to show me what they were for!" Jami defended herself as they both dissolved into laughter. At the time the incident hadn't been at all funny. She'd been afraid she'd get into trouble over it. But Ron had let it slide.

"My neighbors have a very long memory where that night is concerned," Ron observed, clapping a hand to her shoulder. "But enough is enough. Have you had a break yet this afternoon?"

She shook her head quickly. "No, I—"

"I know," he interrupted. "You never take breaks. I remember you always glared at me whenever I suggested it." He flashed her an easy grin. "You always said 'why take a break when we could be out catching some no-good red-handed.' "

"And you always told me that effective police work is one percent good timing and ninety-nine percent luck," she countered dryly. "I'll admit, I was a little idealistic in those days."

"What rookie isn't? Anyway, humor me this once and let's go grab a cup of coffee."

Jami hesitated only an instant. "Thanks, Ron. I'd

like that." She liked Ron, she had from the beginning. They had worked well together and his years of experience had given her an insight into the profession that was too valuable to ignore. When he'd turned her out on her own, her confidence in her own ability was due, in large part, to Ron's expert guidance. Besides, right now she could use a friend.

They climbed the stairs to the main level of the city's government office complex, then strolled across the busy street to a small restaurant. It was a little early for the dinner hour crowd so they were served promptly.

Over two steaming cups of black coffee, she and Ron talked shop for a few minutes. Then Jami inquired about Linda and their two small sons. After that it was inevitable that the subject would turn to her.

"How's your fella?" asked Ron casually.

Jami choked and sputtered on a mouthful of hot coffee, replacing her cup in the saucer with a clatter.

"That good, hmmm?" commented Ron with an amused glint in his eyes. His look changed to a frown as he noted Jami's stricken expression, though she quickly tried to hide it. "Or maybe I should say that bad," he murmured almost to himself. "Something tells me there's trouble in paradise."

"How did you know . . . I was seeing someone?" she finally managed to ask, trying to ignore the sudden churning in her stomach.

Ron looked a little sheepish. "Word travels fast, you know. I heard something about a week in Hawaii?"

Jami groaned softly and closed her eyes. She should have known her remarks in briefing several weeks ago would come back to haunt her. "It just goes to show how the truth can be distorted. It was a *weekend* at the coast, not a week in Hawaii." She stopped and gripped her cup almost convulsively. "Anyway," she added in what she hoped was a nonchalant tone, "it's over, so the rumormongers will have to find someone else to pick on."

Ron smiled sympathetically at her, and Jami realized her efforts to minimize her reaction had failed miserably. "Not that I'm trying to pry or anything," he said, his tone gentle, "but you don't sound too happy about it."

A long silence filled the air before Jami could speak. "It wasn't . . . a mutual decision," she finally said quietly.

Ron leaned forward, his gaze holding hers. "This won't go any further than the two of us, Jami. So if you ever want to talk about it, I'm available."

Jami's eyes met his. "I know that, Ron." A sigh escaped her lips. "But talking won't change what happened, anymore than it will change what's *going* to happen. My job got in the way and—that's that."

Ron studied her for a moment. Then he finally said, "Linda and I had some trouble over that a few years ago."

Her eyes widened. "You did? What happened—" Suddenly she realized how nosy she sounded and clapped a hand over her mouth. "Oh, Ron, I'm sorry," she apologized. "I didn't mean . . ."

"It's okay," he assured her with a smile. "It's not common knowledge, but I don't mind telling you about it if it'll make you feel any better. A lot of it was because of the odd hours and shift changes. For three years in a row I had to work on Christmas and Thanksgiving, plus I was putting in a lot of overtime.

Part of it was the personal safety factor." He shrugged. "It takes a strong and flexible person to handle being married to a police officer, and it requires a lot of patience and understanding on the part of both husband and wife to make a go of it. It's that way in any marriage, but it's especially important to someone in our field." He gave her a wry smile. "Police have one of the highest divorce rates in the country."

"I know," said Jami. She frowned at him thoughtfully. "But obviously you and Linda got through it okay."

"We did," Ron affirmed with a lift of his brows. "But we wouldn't have if both of us hadn't been willing to talk it out, to try to resolve it together." He paused for a second and smiled. "There was never any question of push coming to shove, though. If it had come down to a choice between my career and my wife, I wouldn't be here right now."

"So you would have quit your job," she said slowly. Ron had come through his crisis with no apparent scars. Could she? But then a flicker of dismay stabbed through her. Ron and his wife obviously had love on their side. She and Lance didn't . . . or did they? Of her own love for him, there was no question. But did she dare put a label on his feelings for her, feelings that she knew had once been there for her? Did she dare call it *love*?

Lance's words rushed back into her mind. *Until this afternoon I intended to ask you to marry me.* Suddenly all her doubts began to fade away, relegating themselves to a distant shadowy corner of her mind. Lance wouldn't lie. She knew it . . . she knew it! And he wouldn't even have thought of marriage unless he was very, very sure it was what he wanted.

Her mind drifted back to the weekend at the beach, the night she had given herself to him. Their coupling had been beautiful, truly an act of love. And it certainly hadn't been one-sided. The more she thought about it, the more convinced she became—Lance loved her!

Dazedly she heard Ron's voice. "Anyway," he was saying, "it turned out for the best. I've been a cop for twelve years and it's the only thing I know how to do. At least you've got something to fall back on if you ever decide to quit."

"No, I don't." She frowned as she came back to the present. "This is the only job I've ever held too."

Ron grinned at her, holding up his thumb and index finger so they were only a fraction of an inch apart. "I think you're going senile, lady. You're this close to having a law degree, remember?"

Jami stared at him for a moment in dumbfounded amazement, shock slapping at her in wave after wave. *A law degree.* The phrase repeated itself over and over in her mind. Why hadn't she seen it before? Ron had unwittingly provided her with the answer, and the solution was so simple she couldn't understand why it had eluded her for so long.

Already her mind was racing. She could finish law school in a year and get a job with the District Attorney's office. Surely Lance couldn't object to having a lawyer for his wife. And even though it was a fairly significant career change, it was still in the field she loved and she would be a vital part of the criminal justice system—only a step removed from actually catching someone in the act. Oh, she would miss the excitement of the chase, the satisfaction of being the key instrument in a suspect's apprehension, but the challenge was no less important.

But could she be just as happy as an attorney? It might not have been true three years ago when the police force had crooked its finger at her, but things had changed since then, and so had she. She had, in a sense, sown her wild oats. Yes, she could be happy with Lance beside her.

All she had to do was convince him!

Jami jumped to her feet and reached across the table to smack Ron on the cheek with her lips, heedless of the heads swiveling in their direction at the unexpected display.

"Thank you, Ron! You've just shown me the way back to paradise!"

And with that, she rushed from the restaurant and out into the warm, welcoming sunshine, leaving him sitting alone in the booth, staring after her with his cup suspended halfway to his mouth.

She finished her report in record time and was the first to dash from the conference room after debriefing. Without bothering to change into street clothes, she jumped into her car and started the engine.

The five o'clock traffic over the bridge which led to the hills west of the city was heavy as usual. Jami drummed her fingers impatiently against the wheel as she waited for the cars ahead of her to creep through the traffic signals.

Her jumbled thoughts settled down somewhat as she maneuvered her car onto the highway that wound upward to Lance's house. Yes, what she was doing was right. These last few weeks had been hell, but now she knew she had given up too fast, too easily. She wasn't going to concede defeat so quickly this time. In fact, she wasn't going to concede defeat *at all* if she had anything to say about it.

Somehow she had to convince Lance that nothing—not her job, not his—should be allowed to come between them. The love she nurtured in her heart was too precious to discard so easily, and she could only pray that Lance would feel that way too.

She had talked her way out of a number of volatile situations over the past three years, and she hoped her persuasive tongue wouldn't fail her now, not when she needed it to talk her way into his life again.

She breathed a sigh of relief when she pulled up in front of his house and spotted his Porsche parked in front of the garage doors, but her heart was beating so fast, she feared it would leap through the wall of her chest. Squaring her shoulders, she opened the car door, stepped out, and advanced toward the front entrance.

The gleaming orb of the sun hovered for an instant on the horizon before plunging downward, leaving her in shadow. She shivered in spite of herself. A mixture of doubt and fear rose up inside her for just a fleeting second before she swallowed and lifted a finger to press the doorbell.

It seemed an eternity before the door opened and Lance was standing before her. As always, his aura of virility took her by storm, assaulting her senses and sending her pulses reeling. He looked more dear to her than ever before in black slacks and a cream-colored pullover sweater, but lines of strain were etched into his lean cheeks. He looked tired and drawn, and her heart went out to him. Had he been suffering as much as she?

Apparently not, if his words were anything to go by. "If you're here on official business—although I don't know why you should be—I'm sure you'll understand when I say I'd prefer talking with someone else."

The quiet but cool tone sliced into Jami with the lightning thrust of a knife, but she stood her ground. Now that she'd come this far, she couldn't give up, not without a fight.

"It's personal, Lance," she said quickly. "I—I'd like to talk to you."

Jami's gaze moved over the inscrutable mask that had slipped over his features, lingering on the pulse throbbing in his cheek. She knew she wasn't the only one who was taut and tense as a thin metal wire stretched to its limit. One of them was going to have to give—and soon.

But it wasn't going to be her. She lifted her chin and faced him bravely, but her insides were a quivering mass of gelatin. "This won't take long," she told him. "A few minutes . . . and then we'll see where we stand."

He made an impatient gesture with his hand. "I can't see where anything has changed," he said tiredly. "We've said all there is to be said—"

"No, Lance," she countered swiftly, her breasts rising and falling with each rapid breath. "You said what *you* had to say. *I* didn't." She drew in another breath and waited.

He was silent for so long, she thought her air supply was about to be permanently exhausted. Finally he held the door open wide and motioned her inside.

Jami followed him into the living room. The air was fraught with tension. It was very clear Lance wasn't going to make this easy for her. Suddenly she was far less sure of the outcome of her visit than she'd been an hour ago. Lance looked so . . . so unyielding, she wondered if she'd lost her case even before she was able to present it. An airtight case was what she needed here—would love be enough? It had to be. It just *had* to.

Her nails dug into her palms as she and Lance faced each other. Now that the moment was actually upon her, she didn't know where to begin.

"Lance," she said finally, "I had to come here tonight. You see that, don't you?"

Total silence greeted this announcement, but she made herself go on.

"I've been terribly lonely without you," she said softly, her gaze lingering on his body as he moved away from her and rested his elbow on the mantel above the fireplace. She was a little puzzled at the way he seemed to be avoiding her eyes.

"I—I've missed you."

Again no response. Jami blinked back tears of self-pity but was unable to prevent her voice from catching as she tried again. "Lance, please! Won't you at least listen . . ."

Unknowingly she had moved to him and laid her fingers imploringly on his arm. His muscles tensed at the contact and she drew back as if she'd been seared by a blow torch, her eyes wide with dismay. She was sorely tempted to flee when his gravelly voice halted her.

"I'm listening."

Jami retreated a step, as much for her benefit as his, chewing her lip uncertainly. She suddenly felt as if she were dealing with a stranger—and a very hostile one at that.

"I've come to a decision," she said, choosing her words carefully. So much depended on them! "The last time we saw each other, you seemed to think we were at a dead end, but I think you're wrong, Lance. We have a lot going for us and . . . I don't think we should let it go without at least trying to save what we have." She could feel his eyes on her at last, but couldn't find the courage to meet his look.

"I never thought my work would come between us, but now that it has there's only one thing for me to do." She held up a hand when she saw him shaking his head. "No, let me finish! I've decided to go back to law school and get my degree. I know you said you didn't want me to give up my work for you, but it's my choice." Her small chin wobbled slightly, but she repeated the words with a touch of obstinacy. "It's my choice and it's what I'm going to do."

Lance sighed heavily. "You told me once you'd never considered returning to law school and now you've suddenly changed your mind. The reasons are obvious, but my thinking is still the same. It's too much of a sacrifice—"

"It's not a sacrifice!" Jami wanted to throw her hands into the air in sheer frustration, but she kept them at her sides, only her heaving breasts betraying her agitation. She looked at him then but saw no sign of relenting in his face. What a mess she was making! Nothing was coming out right—nothing!

She lifted a shaky hand to push back a strand of hair from her temple, taking a deep, steadying breath. "Lance," she said in a calmer tone, "I wouldn't even think of going back to law school if I wasn't positive I could be content as an attorney. You call it a sacrifice, I prefer to think of it as a substitute, or a trade. I'm exchanging one career for another. People do it all the time."

"But I brought it about!" he exclaimed harshly. "That's what I can't accept! You're compromising everything you want—"

"I'm not!" she broke in. "I've been perfectly satisfied with my career as a police officer, but I've never seen myself in the same job twenty years from now. Maybe it's a little shortsighted on my part, but it's true. And there was no one but myself to please since my parents never objected, but all that's changed now." Her tone had turned pleading.

"Jami—" he began.

But once the words started to flow, she couldn't seem to stop them. "I'm not doing this just for you, Lance. You told me once that no one can make it alone, that when two people care about each other there's no giving, no taking, only sharing." She took a step closer, lifting her eyes to his face, knowing they revealed her heart. It was a gamble, but she had to take it. "And isn't that what life is all about?" she said softly. "Sharing the joys, the pain, the triumphs, the trouble . . . Alone I'm nothing. With you—only with you—I'm everything."

Her gaze traced the firm contours of his mouth, the mouth that could bring her to the peak of rapture in seconds. Then it moved upward to the straight nose, the thick dark brows, finally reaching the crystal blue depths of his eyes. What she saw there made her heart contract in wonder and surprise as hope burgeoned inside her. He was weakening . . . Oh, yes, he was very definitely weakening!

A soft smile curved her lips as she decided to try a more subtle approach. She placed her fingertips

gainst the firm wall of his chest, pleased at the flare
of desire in his eyes which, though quickly suppressed, proved he was far from immune to her
touch. And if all else failed . . .

Jami tipped her head back to look up at him. "You
know, part of the reason I never considered returning
to law school was because of the expense," she said
softly. "My parents helped me through college, but
after being on my own for so long, I'd have hated to
ask them to help out again." Her fingertips began
lightly tracing a path up and down the front of his
sweater. "Of course, a *husband* helping his *wife*
through law school might be a different matter
entirely. . . ."

She let the sentence trail off, hardly daring to
breathe as she felt Lance's eyes on her face. Her heart
was beating so loudly, she was sure the entire population of Salem could hear it.

"If I had a wife to put through school," he finally
said, one eyebrow lifting slightly as he clasped her
wandering hands, "I probably wouldn't be able to buy
her the Maserati I know she'd love to have." He
paused, then continued in a thoughtful tone, "I'm
not sure she would be willing to give it up."

For just a moment his words were beyond her com-
prehension. Then, as Jami realized what he was saying, a shout of pure joy escaped her and she flung
herself against him, winding her arms around his
neck as if she would never let him go.

"Oh, she would!" Jami's laughter was buoyant and
lilting as she looked up at the man she loved. "She'd
survive somehow. Or better yet, when she was a full-
fledged attorney and earning her own money again,
she would buy it herself."

The look Lance bestowed on her was tenderly indul
gent. "Don't tell me you're going to insist on separat
bank accounts."

"I'm not sure about that." Jami chuckled. "But
definitely won't insist on separate bedrooms!" He
long lashes dropped to fan out on her smooth cream
cheeks as her smile deepened. "Of course, all this tall
about bedrooms and bank accounts is a little prema
ture, don't you think? I mean, considering yo
haven't even asked me to marry you yet."

"I thought *you* asked *me* a minute ago," he teased

"I can see where you might take it that way," sh
admitted, fiddling with the stitching on his sweate
and suddenly feeling a little embarrassed at her own
temerity.

"So my unconventional woman is waiting for a ver
conventional marriage proposal." His tone was light
but there was a wealth of emotion in his eyes as h
tipped her face up to hers. "I love you, Jami. Will yo
marry me?"

"You know I will," was all she was allowed to whis
per sweetly before her mouth was captured by his in
long, slow kiss that reached to her very soul. Sh
could only cling weakly to his shoulders as he sa
down on the sofa and cradled her in his arms.

Lance's tone was husky as he caressed her jawlin
with fingers that weren't entirely steady. "It's scary
you know."

"What is?" She fitted her body more closely to his
as close as the bulk of her uniform and trapping
would allow.

"Loving someone the way I love you."

"I—I know."

"Modest little thing, aren't you?"

Jami laughed shakily, loving him, wanting him, needing him so much it actually hurt inside. Her breath caught in her throat as her gaze caressed his rugged features. Her eyes were suddenly impaled by his, and she read the silent question in the deep blue depths.

"I love you, Lance," she said softly. "I think I knew it all along, but I was afraid of it. I don't think I wanted to be that vulnerable, but it was a losing battle all the way. It was only when you taught me to trust that I knew my feelings were much deeper than I let myself believe."

Her eyes darkened as they probed his. "It scares me to think what might have happened—or rather what might *not* have happened—if I hadn't come here tonight." A shudder ran through her body and her fingers tensed around his neck.

"It would have turned out the same," he reassured her, his breath warm against her cheek. "It might have taken me a few more days to realize it, but I couldn't have been able to stay away much longer. This last month has been sheer torture." His fingers traced the outline of her mouth gently. "Your coming here tonight only hastened the inevitable. I finally admitted to myself what I've been avoiding since we last saw each other. I want you with me, Jami. Always."

"Oh, Lance," she whispered, awed at the tenderness in his voice. She cradled his face in her hands and let her forehead rest against his. "I'm so glad I didn't wait to come. I knew as soon as the solution hit me that it would work, if only I could convince you as well."

"Something tells me your 'solution' was a spur-o
the-moment decision," he observed dryly.

"More or less," she admitted. "But I know it's th
right one and my instincts are usually right on th
money, even if I do say so myself."

"Nevertheless, maybe you should give it some mo
thought." When she shook her head, he added, "I ca
handle it if you decide to stay with the police force.
won't pretend it will be easy, but I know now that li
ing without you isn't living at all. There is somethin
however, I don't want you to give more than a few se
onds of thought to."

"And what's that?" She twined her fingers into th
thick blond strands at his neck, her love for him shi
ing from her eyes.

"When you'll marry me. But I'm warning you, it ha
better be soon or I won't be responsible for carryin
you off to live in sin. Your parents might not b
inclined to look very favorably upon their son-in-la
if you keep me waiting very long." One dark eyebro
quirked upward but his expression was anxious.

Her misty gold eyes closed for a second. She coul
hardly believe this was happening. It was like
dream—a dream she wished would never end.

"How about as soon as we can arrange it? I'd lik
my parents to be there, naturally, but maybe . . . th
end of next week?"

"You won't mind a small informal wedding withou
all the trimmings?"

"Of course not. Something small and intimate wi
suit me just fine."

"Intimate," Lance repeated, his husky tone lendin
a seductive quality to the word. It was clear that hi
thoughts weren't on the wedding itself—but on wha

ame after it! Fascinated, she watched a low flame
gniting in his eyes as his fingers began unfastening
ner gunbelt deftly. "This damn thing has been cut-
ing into my ribs for the last five minutes. Why don't
ve take it off?"

"It is off," she teased as he looped it across the back
of the sofa and turned back to her. "Next you'll be tell-
ng me my badge is digging into your chest and we'll
nave to take off my shirt."

"Among other things." He chuckled and leaned
down to brush his lips against hers, then took her
mouth in a long, passionate kiss that left her yearning
for more. She felt as if she were melting inside, melt-
ng with the warm sweetness of his love. By the time
the soul-wrenching embrace ended, she was bare
from the waist up. Lance had wasted no time in suiting action to words.

"You know," Jami began shakily as his fiery mouth
slowly descended down the sensitive column of her
neck and nibbled a pathway across her collarbone, "I
haven't had any dinner tonight and I'm starving—"

"Oh, Lord, I should have known." Lance groaned as
he lifted his head and gazed down at her with fiery
blue eyes. "Don't tell you I'm going to have to feed you
first!"

A smile tugged at the corners of her mouth. "Well,
maybe afterward," she conceded. "Anyway, if you had
let me finish, I was going to say that I was starving for
you."

"Now that's my kind of talk." He gently squeezed
her.

Jami studied him for a few seconds, her mind wandering for a moment to the future, a future she knew
would be filled with love and happiness. "We're going

to make a great team." She sighed. "Just think, a doctor and a lawyer . . ."

"Dr. and Mrs. Lance Morgan sounds like an unbeatable team to me," he said with a smile. "Or better yet, no doctor, no lawyer—if you decide that's what you want—just you and me."

A warm glow filtered through her body. "I like that," she murmured. *Just you and me.* Such simple words, but they meant so much. A wild elation surged through her veins. She had never been so happy. Only Lance could send a raging torrent of passion coursing through her blood, and only one thing could make her happiness even more complete.

She drew his head down to hers again in sweet surrender, telling him wordlessly of her need to be loved by him—physically, emotionally, in every way that matters to a man and woman who belong together forever.

There was a hungry look in his eyes when he finally released her mouth. The next instant Jami found herself borne upward in strong arms. Lance strode purposefully from the room.

An impish smile curved her lips as she rested her face against his warm shoulder. "Where are we going?"

"To bed, woman, to bed."

"Ah—separate bedrooms?"

"Not tonight, or any other night from now on."

He stopped for a second to open the door to his room and then eased her down to the floor. Jami held tightly to his neck, letting her body glide sensually down the hard length of his, reveling in the feel of his hands on her smooth skin as he tilted her hips so she could feel his burning need for her.

"Is that a promise?" she murmured, already sliding her hands under his sweater. Slim fingers tangled in the soft, curling hair on his chest as she glanced up at him playfully.

A low laugh rumbled deep in his chest before he threaded his fingers in the soft ebony waves of her hair. He turned her face up to his. "That's a promise," he said softly, his velvety tone touching a chord deep within her. "And just to show my good faith, I also promise to love you and only you, forever and always."

And then Jami abandoned herself to the fiery passion that was already drawing them both into a warm, spinning world of love and desire, accepting his words totally and completely.

For this man she loved was many things—but above all, he was a man of his word.

THE EDITOR'S CORNER

The holiday spirit is very much with all of us who work on LOVESWEPT . . . and, feeling like Santa's helpers, we're delighted to tell you about a few of the "surprise packages" you can expect from us next year.

In 1985 Bantam will publish long novels by four of your favorite LOVESWEPT authors. But these books won't be expanded LOVESWEPTS or, for that matter, books of any prescribed format or length. Indeed, the only thing they have in common is that they were written by LOVESWEPT authors! Each novel is different, the author's unique creation, and will be published in Bantam's general list without LOVESWEPT identification. (Never fear, though, that you'll miss these terrific books. I'll be giving you information and lots of reminders about their publication throughout the coming months.)

The first of the four fascinating works by LOVESWEPT authors that you can look forward to enjoying in 1985 is **SUNSET EMBRACE** by Sandra Brown. An ardent love story, a mesmerizing tale of past violence shadowing future happiness, **SUNSET EMBRACE** is a riveting historical set on a wagon train heading for Texas in 1872. A superb storyteller, Sandra has published her contemporary romances under the pen names of Erin St. Clair and Rachel Ryan; her one previous historical romance came out under the name Laura Jordan. **SUNSET EMBRACE** will go on sale during the first two weeks of January. Watch for an excerpt from this historical of spellbinding intensity in the backs of next month's LOVESWEPTS.

Since the other three novels by LOVESWEPT author's won't be published for such a long time, I'll mention them just briefly now and provide more details in months to come. In early April 1985 Iris Johansen's **THE FOREVER DREAM** goes on sale. A fervent love story against a background of a revolutionary scientific breakthrough and political scheming, this high voltage novel is set slightly in the future.

The eagerly anticipated next long work by Sharon and

(continued)

Tom Curtis will appear from Bantam on racks in July 1985. **SUNSHINE AND SHADOW** is so original in its premise and captivating in its execution that we are withholding description of this contemporary romantic novel for several months.

And, then, in November 1985 a remarkable gift goes out to you from Kay Hooper. **THE SUMMER OF THE UNICORN** is a breathtaking piece of romantic magic. Again, we won't reveal more about this novel until closer to publication date.

But, now, let's turn to the reading pleasure you can expect much sooner—namely, the four LOVESWEPTS for you next month.

Witty Billie Green brings us another sparkling romance in **THE COUNT FROM WISCONSIN**, LOVESWEPT #75. From the moment nearsighted cartoonist Kate Sullivan gets dashing Alex Delanore into focus, there is never a dull moment in their courtship. Whether at a magnificent villa in Monte Carlo or speeding through the French countryside after a shady character, Kate and Alex keep one another—and us!—enthralled. But beneath their wild attraction and tender revelations, there is a serious threat to their future together for, it seems, Kate and Alex are caught between two worlds.

Debuting in a new role as published author is our own Elizabeth Barrett with **TAILOR-MADE**, LOVESWEPT #76! A gently evocative love story of a young woman who has shunned the bright lights of Broadway for the tranquil beauty of New Hampshire, **TAILOR-MADE** has a divine hero in actor Daniel Collins. Playing Petruchio in the local summer stock production of *Kiss Me, Kate*, Daniel falls for Chris who is the costumer for the show . . . and finds his path to true love as rough as the one trod by the character he plays.

Nancy Holder strikes again with a thoroughly delightful, highly sensuous, totally off-the-wall love story in **FINDERS KEEPERS**, LOVESWEPT #77. Tender-hearted Allison Jones is a pet detective with a passionate commitment to mystery novels and movies of the 1940's. Heartbreaker David King is San Francisco's Most Eligible Bachelor, the owner of a fleet of limos, and a devoted gadgeteer. It's love at first sight for this unlikely duo . . . followed by a zany, emotion-wrenching clash of life styles that is gripping. I trust that like me you will leave your heart in San Francisco all right—in the roiling fog . . . under the Golden Gate bridge . . . with Allison and David.

What a reception you gave Barbara Boswell's first romance, **LITTLE CONSEQUENCES!** And, following up that successful inaugural bow. Barbara has created a marvelously offbeat romance in **SENSUOUS PERCEPTION,** LOVESWEPT #78. This book could be subtitled The Physicist Encounters the Psychic—but that doesn't really tip you to the fun and the touching emotion you'll experience in reading **SENSUOUS PERCEPTION.** Ashlee Martin has known for years that she's gifted with "second sight" and that as an adoptee she was separated at birth from her twin. Now she's searched out her lost sister Amber and is about to be reunited . . . though even her psychic abilities hadn't forewarned her about the devastating Locke, Amber's foster brother. Yankee Locke may have thought he was an expert in thermodynamic physics—but that was before he encountered Southern belle Ashlee whose mere presence inspires in him a dozen new theories about temperatures rising!

All of us at LOVESWEPT—authors and staff—send you our warmest wishes for a holiday season full of joy! Sincerely,

Carolyn Nichols

Carolyn Nichols
  Editor
LOVESWEPT
Bantam Books, Inc.
666 Fifth Avenue
New York, NY 10103

#1 HEAVEN'S PRICE
By Sandra Brown
Blair Simpson had enclosed herself in the fortress of her dancing, but Sean Garrett was determined to love her anyway. In his arms she came to understand the emotions behind her dancing. But could she afford the high price of love?

#2 SURRENDER
By Helen Mittermeyer
Derry had been pirated from the church by her ex-husband, from under the nose of the man she was to marry. She remembered every detail that had driven them apart—and the passion that had drawn her to him. The unresolved problems between them grew . . . but their desire swept them toward surrender.

#3 THE JOINING STONE
By Noelle Berry McCue
Anger and desire warred within her, but Tara Burns was determined not to let Damon Mallory know her feelings. When he'd walked out of their marriage, she'd been hurt.

Damon had violated a sacred trust, yet her passion for him was as breathtaking as the Grand Canyon.

#4 SILVER MIRACLES
By Fayrene Preston
Silver-haired Chase Colfax stood in the Texas moonlight, then took Trinity Ann Warrenton into his arms. Overcome by her own needs, yet determined to have him on her own terms, she struggled to keep from losing herself in his passion.

#5 MATCHING WITS
By Carla Neggers
From the moment they met, Ryan Davis tried to outmaneuver Abigail Lawrence. She'd met her match in the Back Bay businessman. And Ryan knew the Boston lawyer was more woman than any he'd ever encountered. Only if they vanquished their need to best the other could their love triumph.

#6 A LOVE FOR ALL TIME
By Dorothy Garlock
A car crash had left its marks on Casey Farrow's beauty. So what were Dan

Murdock's motives for pursuing her? Guilt? Pity? Casey had to choose. She could live with doubt and fear . . . or learn a lesson in love.

#7 A TRYST WITH MR. LINCOLN?

By Billie Green
When Jiggs O'Malley awakened in a strange hotel room, all she saw were the laughing eyes of stranger Matt Brady . . . all she heard were his teasing taunts about their "night together" . . . and all she remembered was nothing! They evaded the passions that intoxicated them until . . . there was nowhere to flee but into each other's arms.

#8 TEMPTATION'S STING

By Helen Conrad
Taylor Winfield likened Rachel Davidson to a Conus shell, contradictory and impenetrable. Rachel battled for independence, torn by her need for Taylor's embraces and her impassioned desire to be her own woman. Could they both succumb to the temptation of the tropi-

cal paradise and still be true to their hearts?

#9 DECEMBER 32nd . . . AND ALWAYS

By Marie Michael
Blaise Hamilton made her feel like the most desirable woman on earth. Pat opened herself to emotions she'd thought buried with her late husband. Together they were unbeatable as they worked to build the jet of her late husband's dreams. Time seemed to be running out and yet—would ALWAYS be long enough?

#10 HARD DRIVIN' MAN

By Nancy Carlson
Sabrina sensed Jacy in hot pursuit, as she maneuvered her truck around the racetrack, and recalled his arms clasping her to him. Was he only using her feelings so he could take over her trucking company? Their passion knew no limits as they raced full speed toward love.

#11 BELOVED INTRUDER

By Noelle Berry McCue
Shannon Douglas hated

Michael Brady from the moment he brought the breezes of life into her shadowy existence. Yet a specter of the past remained to torment her and threaten their future. Could he subdue the demons that haunted her, and carry her to true happiness?

#12 HUNTER'S PAYNE
By Joan J. Domning
P. Lee Payne strode into Karen Hunter's office demanding to know why she was stalking him. She was determined to interview the mysterious photographer. She uncovered his concealed emotions, but could the secrets their hearts confided protect their love, or would harsh daylight shatter their fragile alliance?

#13 TIGER LADY
By Joan J. Domning
Who *was* this mysterious lover she'd never seen who courted her on the office computer, and nicknamed her Tiger Lady? And could he compete with Larry Hart, who came to repair the computer

and stayed to short-circuit her emotions? How could she choose between poetry and passion—between soul and Hart?

#14 STORMY VOWS
By Iris Johansen
Independent Brenna Sloan wasn't strong enough to reach out for the love she needed, and Michael Donovan knew only how to take—until he met Brenna. Only after a misunderstanding nearly destroyed their happiness, did they surrender to their fiery passion.

#15 BRIEF DELIGHT
By Helen Mittermeyer
Darius Chadwick felt his chest tighten with desire as Cygnet Melton glided into his life. But a prelude was all they knew before Cyg fled in despair, certain she had shattered the dream they had made together. Their hearts had collided in an instant; now could they seize the joy of enduring love?

#16 A VERY RELUC-TANT KNIGHT
By Billie Green
A tornado brought them together in a storm cel-

lar. But Maggie Sims and Mark Wilding were anything but perfectly matched. Maggie wanted to prove he was wrong about her. She knew they didn't belong together, but when he caressed her, she was swept up in a passion that promised a lifetime of love.

#17 TEMPEST AT SEA
By Iris Johansen
Jane Smith sneaked aboard playboy-director Jake Dominic's yacht on a dare. The muscled arms that captured her were inescapable—and suddenly Jane found herself agreeing to a month-long cruise of the Caribbean. Jane had never given much thought to love, but under Jake's tutelage she discovered its magic . . . and its torment.

#18 AUTUMN FLAMES
By Sara Orwig
Lily Dunbar had ventured too far into the wilderness of Reece Wakefield's vast Chilean ranch; now an oncoming storm thrust her into his arms . . . and he refused to let her go. Could he lure her, step by seductive step, away from the life she had forged for herself, to find her real home in his arms?

#19 PFARR LAKE AFFAIR
By Joan J. Domning
Leslie Pfarr hadn't been back at her father's resort for an hour before she was pitched into the lake by Eric Nordstrom! The brash teenager who'd made her childhood a constant torment had grown into a handsome man. But when he began persuading her to fall in love, Leslie wondered if she was courting disaster.

#20 HEART ON A STRING
By Carla Neggers
One look at heart surgeon Paul Houghton Welling told JoAnna Radcliff he belonged in the stuffy society world she'd escaped for a cottage in Pigeon Cove. She firmly believed she'd never fit into his life, but he set out to show her she was wrong. She was the puppet master, but he knew how to keep her heart on a string.

#21 THE SEDUCTION OF JASON
By Fayrene Preston
On vacation in Martinique, Morgan Saunders found Jason Falco. When a misunderstanding drove him away, she had to win him back. Morgan acted as a seductress, to tempt him to return; she sent him tropical flowers to tantalize him; she wrote her love in letters twenty feet high—on a billboard that echoed the words in her heart.

#22 BREAKFAST IN BED
By Sandra Brown
For all Sloan Fairchild knew, Hollywood had moved to San Francisco when mystery writer Carter Madison stepped into her bed-and-breakfast inn. In his arms the forbidden longing that throbbed between them erupted. Sloan had to choose—between her love for him and her loyalty to a friend . . .

#23 TAKING SAVANNAH
By Becky Combs
The Mercedes was headed straight for her! Cassie hurled a rock that smashed the antique car's taillight. The price driver Jake Kilrain exacted was a passionate kiss, and he set out to woo the Southern lady, Cassie, but discovered that his efforts to conquer the lady might end in his own surrender . . .

#24 THE RELUCTANT LARK
By Iris Johansen
Her haunting voice had earned Sheena Reardon fame as Ireland's mournful dove. Yet to Rand Challon the young singer was not just a lark but a woman whom he desired with all his heart. Rand knew he could teach her to spread her wings and fly free, but would her flight take her from him or into his arms forever?

#25 LIGHTNING THAT LINGERS
By Sharon and Tom Curtis
He was the Cougar Club's star attraction, mesmerizing hundreds of women with hips that swayed in the provocative motions

of love. Jennifer Hamilton offered her heart to the kindred spirit, the tender poet in him. But Philip's wordly side was alien to her, threatening to unravel the magical threads binding them . . .

#26 ONCE IN A BLUE MOON
By Billie Green
Arlie was reckless, wild, a little naughty—but in the nicest way! Whenever she got into a scrape, Dan was always there to rescue her. But this time Arlie wanted a very *personal* bailout that only *he* could provide. Dan never could say no to her. After all, the special favor she wanted was his own secret wish—wasn't it?

#27 THE BRONZED HAWK
By Iris Johansen
Kelly would get her story even if it meant using a bit of blackmail. She'd try anything to get inventor-genius Nick O'Brien to take her along in his experimental balloon. Nick had always trusted his

fate to the four winds and the seven seas . . . until a feisty lady clipped his wings by losing herself in his arms . . .

#28 LOVE, CATCH A WILD BIRD
By Anne Reisser
Daredevil and dreamer, Bree Graeme collided with Cane Taylor on her family's farm—and there was an instant intimacy between them. Bree's wild years came to a halt, for when she looked into Cane's eyes, she knew she'd found love at last. But what price freedom to dare when the man she loved could rest only as she lay safe in his arms?

#29 THE LADY AND THE UNICORN
By Iris Johansen
Janna Cannon scaled the walls of Rafe Santine's estate, determined to appeal to the man who could save her animal preserve. She bewitched his guard dogs, then cast a spell over him as well. She offered him a gift he'd never dared risk reaching for before—but could he trust

his emotions enough to open himself to her love?

#30 WINNER TAKE ALL
By Nancy Holder
Holly Johnson was a powerful presence at the office, an unstoppable force on the racquetball court, and too much woman for the men she knew . . . until Dick DeWitt came into her life. A battle of wills and wits ensued, and to the victors the spoils were happiness and love.

#31 THE GOLDEN VALKYRIE
By Iris Johansen
Private detective Honey Winston had been duped into invading Prince Rubinoff's hotel suite. But behind the facade of the gossip columns' "Lusty Lance" she found an artist filled with longing. Would the gift of her love allow Lance to escape his gilded prison?

#32 C.J.'S FATE
By Kay Hooper
C.J. Adams had been teased about her lack of interest in men. On a ski trip with her friends she embraced a stranger, pretending they were secret lovers. Astonished at his reaction, she tried to nip their romance in the bud. But she'd met her match in a man who could answer her witty remarks and arouse in her a passionate need.

#33 THE PLANTING SEASON
By Dorothy Garlock
Iris had poured her energies into the family farm and the appearance of John Lang was unexpected. Suddenly the land was theirs to share. John wanted to prove his dedication and his feelings for Iris. But when disaster struck, it forced a confrontation that risked everything and taught Iris that only learning to grow together would bring them a harvest of love.

#34 FOR THE LOVE A SAMI
By Fayrene Preston
When heiress Sami Adkinson was arrested for demonstrating to save the seals, she begged attorney Daniel Parker-St. James

to bail her out. Daniel was smitten, soon cherishing Sami and protecting her from her fears. But holding onto Sami he found, was like trying to hug quicksilver . . .

#35 THE TRUSTWORTHY REDHEAD
By Iris Johansen
When Sabrina Courtney was hired to deliver birthday wishes to Alex ben Rashid, she wasn't warned that he had a weakness for redheads. From the moment he saw her, he wanted to possess her. Could a man who was used to getting what he wanted learn to trust the woman he loved?

#36 A TOUCH OF MAGIC
By Carla Neggers
A tragedy had made Sarah Blackstone president of her family's corporation. Promising herself one last fling, she bicycled to visit the Blackstones' old farm, only to find Brad "Magic" Craig, quarterback of the New York Novas. Brad tried to brand her as just another fan bent on seducing the Superbowl he-

ro, but was the emotion between them real?

#37 IRRESISTIBLE FORCES
By Marie Michael
Shane McCallister considered the assignment of interviewing Nick Rutledge, the hero of the silver screen, a demotion. She resented having to profile a vain and shallow star. But she had her expectations shattered. Nick was intelligent, sensitive, and concerned about people and the land. And so the story she wrote had an irresistibly happy ending.

#38 TEMPORARY ANGEL
By Billie Green
When an explosion trapped Angie Jones and Senator Sam Clements in a cave for hours alone, her resistance to his charm weakened. But surely a Senator couldn't succeed if he were linked with a controversial writer like her! Angie hadn't counted on a filibuster—as Sam held fast to the angel who showed him the stars from close up . . .

trenchcoat changed everything! But the lovers weren't lost to an uncaring world . . . for her life was threatened by a man from the past she couldn't recall . . .

#44 NO RED ROSES
By Iris Johansen
When singer Rex Brody took Tamara Ledford in his arms, he knew the lady he'd been singing to all along was no longer a fantasy. But could he convince her that his feelings were sincere? Tamara rebelled, aching to return to her greenhouse and her precious herbs and flowers. Then Rex showered her with blossoms . . . but there were no red roses . . .

#45 THAT OLD FEELING
By Farene Preston
When she heard the waves crashing against the Baja coast, Lisa Saxon felt them echo within her heart. And when she turned to find Christopher, her ex-husband, her pulse quickened in frustration and desire. Could they dare to be honest, and make it for keeps this time?

#46 SOMETHING DIFFERENT
By Kay Hooper
Like her name, Gypsy had always preferred to roam the world at will, writing her books and loving the heroes who filled her dreams. But then architect Chase Mitchell slipped inside her heart to fulfill her fantasies. Gypsy and Chase resisted the happy ending the dream demanded— until a wily feline matchmaker found the keys to their love.

#47 THE GREATEST SHOW ON EARTH
By Nancy Holder
Melinda Franklin had a dream that wouldn't die: To keep hers an old-fashioned circus. Banker Evan Kessel arrived to review her loan application and ended up courting Melinda in the midst of her circus "family." How could a woman whose right palm revealed a heartline as big as the Grand Canyon resist him?

AN EXQUISITELY ROMANTIC NOVEL UNLIKE
ANY OTHER LOVE STORY YOU HAVE EVER READ

Chase
the Moon

by
Catherine Nicholson

For Corrie Modena, only one man shares her dreams, a stranger whom she has never met face to face and whom she knows only as "Harlequin." Over the years, his letters sustain her—encouraging, revealing, increasingly intimate. And when Corrie journeys to Paris to pursue her music, she knows that she will also be searching for her beloved Harlequin. . . .

Buy CHASE THE MOON, on sale November 15, 1984, wherever Bantam paperbacks are sold, or use the handy coupon below for ordering:

A Dazzling New Novel

Scents

by
Johanna Kingsley

They were the fabulous Jolays, half sisters, bound by blood but not by love. Daughters of an outstanding French perfumer whose world had collapsed, now they are bitter rivals, torn apart by their personal quests for power. It was the luminous Vie who created an empire, but it was the sensuous, rebellious Marty who was determined to control it. No matter what the cost, she would conquer Vie's glittering world and claim it as her own . . .

Buy SCENTS, on sale December 15, 1984, wherever Bantam paperbacks are sold, or use the handy coupon below for ordering:

A TOWERING, ROMANTIC SAGA BY
THE AUTHOR OF
LOVE'S WILDEST FIRES

HEARTS
of
FIRE

by Christina Savage

For Cassie Tryon, Independence Day, 1776, signals a
different kind of upheaval—the wild, unstoppable rebel-
lion of her heart. For on this day, she will meet a
stranger—a legendary privateer disguised in clerk's
clothes, a mysterious man come to do secret, patriot's
business with her father . . . a man so compelling that she
knows her life will never be the same for that meeting. He
is Lucas Jericho—outlaw, rebel, avenger of his family's
fate at British hands, a man who is dangerous to love . . .
and impossible to forget.

Buy HEARTS OF FIRE, on sale November 1, 1984, wherever Bantam paperbacks are sold, or use the handy
coupon below for ordering:

A Stirring Novel of Destinies
Bound by Unquenchable Passion

SUNSET EMBRACE

by Sandra Brown

Fate threw Lydia Russell and Ross Coleman, two untamed outcasts, together on a Texas-bound wagon train. On that wild road, they fought the breathtaking desire blazing between them, while the shadows of their enemies grew longer. As the train rolled west, danger drew ever closer, until a showdown with their pursuers was inevitable. Before it was over, Lydia and Ross would face death . . . the truth about each other . . . and the astonishing strength of their love.

Buy SUNSET EMBRACE, on sale January 15, 1985 wherever Bantam paperbacks are sold, or use the handy coupon below for ordering:

# LOVESWEPT

Love Stories you'll never forget by authors you'll always remember

LOVESWEPT

Love Stories you'll never forget
by authors you'll always remember